For Mom

CHAPTER 1

Thatcher writhed on the grimy, hard, cold stone floor of their prison cell with what he thought were believable contortions. It had been hours since they had been brought to their tiny prison, and it looked as if the Italians would take their own merry time in getting around to doing something about their unexpected guests. Thatcher was merely taking it upon himself to speed up the process.

Nothing had gone quite as planned since that moment in Dover when a tantalizing stranger had sat on the bench next to him in the seedy pub along the wharf, draping herself across him and whispering sweet plans of espionage into his ear. As a mercenary, he had experienced a few different situations in his life, but none as interesting as that moment. But he hadn't known then that he and the evocative stranger would end up on a ship, bound for a destination they did not know, spending days sequestered in the cargo berth as they traversed the choppy ocean, hoping the ship's captain would not find them out, decide stowaways were not worth the extra nuisance, and toss them overboard. It was about time Thatcher took matters into his own hands.

Katharine Cavanaugh, the Countess of Stirling, courtesy of her War Office cover, jumped right into the game, her incredible acting skills kicking into motion before he had even hit the floor. He hoped by not telling her his plan, her actions would be more authentic. But having seen her in play, he doubted she could get any better at what she did. As he began his first round of tremors, she knelt by his side, her voice raised in a scream of indecipherable terror. He dared to peek once, just to see what she was doing and enjoy a bit of the show, when he saw her kneeling there, her tattered bar wench costume barely clinging to her lush curves, the bodice a display for her ample bosom, her thick brown hair falling in waves around her face, framing her square features with soft velocity. He forced his eyes shut.

And soon running footsteps echoed down the passageway.

The staccato of rapidly moving footfalls grew more hurried the closer the sounds came to their cell, and Thatcher knew Kate's screams drew them in like sheep to the slaughter. He hoped the guards would get there quickly. He wasn't sure how much convulsing he could do without repeating his repertoire. But soon he heard the metal clinking of keys going into a lock, and Kate's screams became focused in the direction of the door. Soon there was a thud, and the unmistakable screeching of a metal door swinging open, and then --

"Don't touch him!" Kate yelled in English, her accent shifting like a mirage on the desert. It became something it could not be and yet was with absolute certainty.

Now Thatcher truly did wish to open his eyes just to see the sound as it escaped the full lips of the woman who so captivated him from the moment she came to rest on his lap in that pub in Dover. It was an accent unlike he had ever heard before, but he instantly knew that she was someone to be obeyed.

The footfalls stopped, and Thatcher almost stopped moving as well, so enraptured he was by the performance he could not see.

"Can you not see what is happening?" Kate went on, and Thatcher wanted to inform her that he, in fact, could not see what was happening. But he lay there, moving his body in undulating tremors.

He wasn't sure what happened then , but there was inde-cipherable muttering in what must have been Italian, and then Kate's harsh, "Silence!"

The noise about him ceased, and suddenly, a pair of hands were on him. He would have jerked away if the touch had not become so familiar to him in the past few days they had been at sea.

Kate's sure hands gripped his head, pulling his upper body into her lap. He felt the brush of her skirts against his cheeks, smelled the salt from the sea on her skin.

And for a second, he was lost. Lost in the feel of her grip, in the smell of her body, in the nearness of her heat. For days, he had done nothing but exist in her company, her guardian as they crossed the Channel and made their way through the Strait of Gibraltar. And through all of that, he had done nothing to question his respect of her person, and now, he lay with his head in her lap, his body pulled against hers like he had longed to do during their entire sea voyage.

"He is having a vision!" Kate cried, and he felt one of her hands leave him. He pictured her swooping said hand into the air with dramatic flair.

He was having a what?

"A vision!" Kate cried again, and Thatcher assumed one of the Italians had done something to question her statement.

"Do you not know who this is?" she continued. "It is Mick Brody of the Brodys of Galway. He is a seer of the old ways and the ancient wisdom. He sees something now before us. Speak, Mick, speak of what you see!"

What he saw?

He saw the backs of his eyelids or perhaps nothing at all. He really wasn't sure how that worked. And he couldn't speak if he continued to shake the way he was, so he did the only thing of which he could think. He stopped.

Sitting upright in one fluid motion, he worked the muscles of his abdomen as he swung his arms up toward the moist ceiling of their prison. He felt his hair swing along the sides of his head, but he didn't dare move to shake it free from his face. He was supposed to be in a trance after all, a vision encompassing all of his senses.

"Oh great sacred one, you come before me again!" He tried to make his accent as alluring as Kate's, knowing he could not carry off an Irish brogue if someone paid him to do so. He had been through Dublin a time or two, and he knew he would not be fooling anyone. So instead, he went for the slightly vague, if terribly curious, unknown lilt. He thought he had done a fairly accurate job when suddenly a rush of intake breath swept along his right side, and a collective step backward sounded in his ear.

He continued. "You have blessed me with yet another of your precious visions, and I thank you, oh sacred one."

He suddenly wished he had paid attention when his mama had dragged him to church with Thomas. If only he had had the sense to pay attention to her religious, dramatic ways, he may have something to say at this moment. But in all fairness, he never expected to be in such a situation when he was ten years old. Well, at least the part about having to pretend to have some sort of divine observance. He would not be so bold as to suggest he hadn't thought about having his head in the lap of a bar wench.

"I see what you have come here to show me. I see what you have wrought."

Here he quickly pulled his arms against his chest, doubling over as he held his arms against himself. He felt his hair drape across his eyes, and in that moment, he peeked, taking in the appearance of the guard nearest him. Continuing the fluid motion, he swung his head back, spreading his arms wide to the ceiling above him.

"It is him you seek!" he shouted, and with one outstretched hand, he extended a single index finger to indicate the guard he had stolen a glimpse of in his hastily concealed peek. "It is him. He with the matted beard. He with the green eyes of lust and envy. He with the scuffed boots of disrespect. You wish him--"

He was unable to finish the sentence as the entire armed guard descended on their chosen brethren. A tug on his shoulder had him opening his eyes and dropping his arms as Kate struggled to pull him away from the fray. The guard of Italian soldiers, perhaps six or seven of them, had all piled into a corner. The unfortunate soul Thatcher had seen when he had chanced a glimpse of the men was invisible in the crush, but Thatcher knew he lay at the very center of the throbbing mass of religiously terrified men.

"Well, I reckon our welcome is worn thin. Shall we see to getting ourselves out of this place?" Thatcher said as he stood and brushed carelessly at his pants. He quickly pulled Kate to her feet, but the movement was perhaps abrupt as she bounced unexpectedly against him. For a moment, he wished she would do it again, but in the back of his mind, his internal safety mechanism kept bumping at his conscience, telling him to keep moving. And so he did, relinquishing the closeness of a delectably warm Countess of Stirling.

"But--" Kate began, but he was already moving her in the direction of the now open cell door, abandoned by the Italian guard engaged in apprehending one of their own. She didn't finish her sentence but followed willfully behind him, her height affording a stride nearly equal to his.

He quickly found his way back through the passages the guards had taken when they had removed them from the officer's quarters where they had been interrogated. Soon Thatcher heard the sounds of the world above, and a ray of sunlight bounced down a flight of stairs that came into view as soon as they rounded a third corner of crumbling stone. He did not have to drag Kate behind him, for at the sight of the stairs, her pace quickened to match his.

Sunlight struck him full in the face as he emerged from the grated door of their prison and into the bustling streets of a port city on the Mediterranean Sea. As soon as his feet hit the cobblestone, he dodged to the left, tucking Kate behind him as a cart laden with crates of olives passed just in front of the toes of his boots.

Kate pressed against his back, her heart beating a tattoo into the muscles there. He felt a corresponding ripple in other parts of his body and swallowed to focus on the task at hand. They needed to get away from the prison and the authorities that had brought them there. They needed to find a place to hide until they could regain their composure and perhaps find some suitable clothes for Kate, even if she did make a fetching bar wench.

"Get in the cart."

Thatcher looked quickly to his right at the cart that had just passed them as if the voice had come from the olives themselves. But knowing that could not be right, he looked up to the bench. A small, squat man, thick through the middle and thin at the limbs hovered like a forgotten presence on the worn bench of the rickety cart. Surely, it was him who had spoken the words, for in the bustle around them, no other person was close enough to utter such words with such clarity for Thatcher to hear.

And the man had spoken in English.

Thatcher turned long enough to scoop Kate into his arms, and together, he launched them into the back of the cart, landing precariously between the rows of olive crates. The cart lurched forward before his body settled onto the boards of the cart, and Kate's unbelievable warmth came to rest against the full length of his body. He let out a rush of air that had nothing to do with escape and possible pursuit. It was a rush of pure male lust that exited his lungs and with it, his last hope of keeping his hands off of the woman who now lay sprawled across his body.

She struggled against him, likely trying to gain purchase and find a space for herself where there was none in the cart. Thatcher stilled her with his hands a little too far down on her hips, the tattered skirts of her costume having ridden up to her knees, trapping her legs between his. Her head came up, and he stared into hazel eyes, murky with a mystery he could not wait to solve.

"Better relax, my friend. I think we're going for a ride," he said, letting his hands slip just a little more down her hips.

And that was when he saw it. The flash of responding desire in those hazel depths that brought a corresponding flicker from his own awareness.

She wanted him.

She may not know that she wanted him, but there, pressed against each other between crates of olives in a cart that was likely to collapse before safely rescuing them away from their captors, driven by a man they did not know and who could possibly have nefarious connections, Matthew

Thatcher knew that a lusty bar wench wanted him. And not just any lusty bar wench.

Katharine Cavanaugh, the Countess of Stirling.

And for the first time in days, he smiled.

CHAPTER 2

The cart bumped beneath them, and Kate felt each of the dips and mounds as the ancient vehicle threatened to buckle under them. And Thatcher lay there, his hands slipping along the sides of her body with a purpose she knew he thought she did not suspect. And in all of it, she stared into the startling blue eyes that dared her to blink. But as she lay there, mesmerized by his gaze, enraptured by his touch, practicality reared its ugly head, and the War Office trained spy in her took over.

"Who is this gentleman?" she whispered, bringing her head closer to Thatcher's than prudence may have dictated at that moment.

Thatcher wiggled his eyebrows, his smile melting across his features.

"I haven't the faintest idea, but he seemed to be rather convenient when we needed him," he said. "A vision? That was your moment of inspiration?"

Kate blinked at him beneath her. "Did you have a better idea?"

He shrugged, the movement adjusting his hard body

against hers in a way that caused her heart to flutter. "I reckon not," he replied.

Kate wanted to sigh her feelings of frustration with both Thatcher's judgment of her actions and their current predicament of trusting a stranger, but she knew it would do her little good. She was finding Thatcher's American ways odd but adamant. A part of her admired that while another was frustrated by it. She instead went back to the most relevant topic at that moment.

"So we're trusting him with our lives when he could be now returning us to our enemies?"

"Oh, I wouldn't do that," said the man on the bench, his voice thick with the accent of the region, "I would have no cause to. The authorities here are not very giving in the exchange of infidels."

Kate noted how articulate he was and pondered where he had learned such exquisite English. Although his accent was thick, his words were accurate, and she caught herself looking up at him, her eyes squinting in the harsh light of the Mediterranean sun. She must have pulled her head up too far though, because soon she felt Thatcher's hand along the nape of her neck, pulling her back down. She thought for a moment of resisting, of pulling herself away from him, but first, there was no room in the cart for her to go anywhere but lay on top of him, and second, his touch felt far too scandalous to resist.

That last bit may have been improper, but she argued it like this. They had been carrying out a sanctioned mission of the War Office when their objectives had been compromised, and they had been forced to improvise. Such improvisation had led to their current circumstances of being marooned in a hostile territory with little to no hope of escape. If she wanted to enjoy, if but for a moment, the sensual touch of a gentleman she respected, she would do so.

"You have a rather generous bosom, Kate Cavanaugh," Thatcher said, just as she relaxed against him, her head finding a spot on his shoulder as the cart moved along the cobblestone streets of the port city.

But even as her head touched his shoulder, she jerked it back up at his words.

"I beg your--"

"It is just a statement of fact, little lady. Nothing untoward meant by it. I just hope there's room in this cart for it, is all."

She wanted to be angry with him. She wanted to scold him for his impolite speak, but when she truly thought of it, she did have a large bosom. It was, as he had said, fact after all. And she suddenly felt like laughing.

"Well, I hope you can find it in your giving Christian self to find the room for it," she responded instead, returning her head to his shoulder.

She could almost hear his heart beating as she lay there, her ear pressed against his chest, but the noises of the cart and the activities of the port drowned out almost everything else. She closed her eyes and concentrated on the heat of his body, the touch of his skin and the feel of his breath under the hand on his chest. She had never been this close to a man, she realized. And with that realization, a flicker of apprehension spread through her.

She shouldn't be having a reaction to him at all.

Her whole life had been centered around her career as a spy. From the very first time her father took her aside and explained the situation, she had had only one thought in her mind, one goal to strive for. She had never doubted or wavered since that moment. And her devotion had precluded the normal events in a woman's life such as a husband and family. She had never once noticed their absence from her life until that very moment, when she lay sprawled across an American mercenary in the back of an olive cart. The confusion needled at her until she resolutely pushed it away, focusing on their objective, which at the moment was to get as far away from the men who had apprehended them as possible.

The sounds of the port began to fade. Dock hands crying out instructions for loading cargo, fishmongers selling their wares, and the incessant flap and call of sea birds as they scavenged for food began to drift from her range of hearing. There was only the cart now, creaking and squelching as they made their way further out of Naples.

And there it was.

The unmistakable thump of Thatcher's heart. It was a tremendous sound against her ear, and the hand she rested on his chest flinched as if his heart may come right through his person and into her palm. The idea moved her. The thought of holding his heart in her hand brought all sorts of silly nostalgia to her mind, instigated by all of the romantic novels she had deigned worthy of her attention. She should have known her mother to be correct when she had labeled such novels as trivial at best and at worst, terribly persuasive. For Kate suddenly thought of herself as the stricken heroine of such a tale and Thatcher her admirable, if troubled, hero. The image did not sit right on Thatcher as there was nothing troubled about him, but Kate thought it likely she could portray stricken with agreeable flare.

The confusion she had only moments before pushed from her mind rose up again. She swallowed.

"Where are we going?" she suddenly whispered to Thatcher, feeling overcome by her sudden fanciful thoughts, needing to distract herself with a cold, jarring dose of reality.

They were stranded in Naples, for God's sake, the armpit of Napoleon's control, if she were to be more graphic. Napoleon himself may not be in residence, but his brother-in-law had taken no qualms to running the show in his esteemed in-law's absence. Kate wanted to be sick at the thought. Power was simply too much for people sometimes, she was afraid.

"I haven't a clue," Thatcher said beneath her.

"To my farm. It is only over the hills a ways," said the man on the bench.

Kate tilted her head to catch a glimpse of him. The slumped man seemed even more stooped than he had earlier, his soft cap rounding on his head. Tufts of thick, wiry gray hair protruded from the peaks of his ears, and when he turned his head to peer about him, she could see the rounded bulbous of his nose and the soft contours of his wrinkled cheeks. But his mouth appeared relaxed in what may have been a smile if Kate could see it better, and his eyes squinted into the sun as if they looked forward to it every day.

"A farm?" Thatcher said, and she became aware of the fact that he had grown suddenly tense beneath her.

The cart did not allow for much relaxation, but Thatcher had never been one to disappoint her when it came to embracing a leisurely lifestyle. But she suddenly felt the muscles of his body, extending along her own, coil and bunch as if in anticipation of a fight she did not know about.

"Thatcher?" she said, softer now and closer to his ear, as she rested against him once more.

"I dislike farms," was all he said, but he remained tense for the remainder of their journey.

The cart made one more terrific bump before settling to a stop in what Kate hoped was the yard of the farm their unknown rescuer had mentioned. She would have sat up to see her surroundings, but the lack of space in the cart would have meant she would be sitting in Thatcher's lap. As much as the thought excited her, she also did not think Thatcher would welcome it in his current state.

She raised her head to look at his face to discern if she

could read anything more into his sudden state of discomfort. She would have thought if he were to be uncomfortable at any part in their journey, it would have come before then . Perhaps when she, a perfect stranger, had sat on his lap in a pub in Dover and explained to him who their target was. Or perhaps when they had boarded a ship only to discover its destination was an enemy held country. Or perhaps when they had found themselves hiding amongst the cargo to avoid detection as stowaways, he may have felt a twinge of discomfort. But through all of that he had remained utterly jovial, his face quick to spread into a smile of simple and pure delight.

And now he chose to be concerned? About a farm? She imagined an idyllic farm on the English countryside with pigs and sheep and cows and could not find anything concerning about cows.

She would have questioned his state but feared he may have an aversion to cows or something equally as humiliating and did not want to draw attention to the fact. If Matthew Thatcher had a dislike of farm residences, then she would not be the one to make a point of it. But she would make sure he was all right in exiting their conveyance.

"Thatcher, would it be all right if I--"

Before she finished the sentence, he sat up, drawing her carefully across his lap, his arms loose about her waist as she settled once more in the position she had first assumed when introducing herself as bar wench. Her face came even with his, and his blond curls, now ragged with dirt and sweat, swung close around his face. She stared for a moment, taking in the beauty of his rugged looks, encased in a filth she should have found disagreeable and yet found tantalizingly resplendent. English gentlemen never favored such a state of unkempt. The idea that an American could embrace such a development was strikingly foreign and equally as desirable.

"I guess it would be then ," she said when she found her voice.

Thatcher looked about them, and it was then that she realized she should have been doing the same. They may have been out of prison, but they were still surrounded by the enemy, whoever that was in this country.

They were, in fact, in the front yard of a farm, a working olive farm it appeared to be. The farm nestled back into a grove along the hillside, the olive trees rising up and away from the squat farmhouse before them like the collar of a monarch, regal and fine, daunting and commanding. The scene was breathtaking even before Kate turned her head to take in the opposite view, the sight of the port spread out below them, and the majestic blue of the sea rippled out until the eye could see no more. She felt her breath catch in her throat at the sight of it, and Thatcher's hand at her back began to make small, circular soothing motions. She felt childish only for a moment until the beauty of it overcame her, and she turned to find the old man who had rescued them.

He stood at the back of the cart, his hat in one hand as he scratched at the crown of his head, his wiry, gray hair flapping amongst his movements as he surveyed the same view she had just done.

"It's beautiful," she said, her voice thick with emotion.

The old man turned to her, and for the first time, Kate took in his entire appearance at once. He was indeed short with a strong chest and stomach with arms grown willowy with age. His face was soft pockets of wrinkled flesh, tanned and creased by the rays of the sun. His eyes were an unknowable murky color but shined with an enthusiasm Kate felt in her bones.

"It is, isn't it?" the man replied, and she was reminded again of the man's excellent English.

"It is," Kate agreed.

She turned to Thatcher, sitting quietly beneath her. He still looked at the farm behind them, having not turned his head toward the brilliant view of the sea. She wanted to prompt him to look out beyond them, but there was something in the set of his jaw, the lines around his eyes, and the small tick in his cheek that stopped her. Something truly bothered Matthew Thatcher, and his uneasiness made her uneasy. She coughed as if to right the situation enough to move them forward.

"Well, then , Mr. Thatcher, I suppose we must get ourselves out of this gentleman's cart," she said, wiggling to slide off of Thatcher's legs and hopefully find herself standing on the firm ground outside of the cart. It was only a hope, she knew, as she found herself catapulting out of the cart when her skirts suddenly came free from Thatcher's legs, and instead of standing, she crumpled in a heap at the end of the cart, her ample bosom finding the hard packed dirt of the yard with killing focus. The old man bent quickly, taking her arm in his as he helped her up.

She thanked him and then turned to Thatcher.

"Thatcher?" she prompted as he continued to stare at the farm.

She followed the direction of his gaze but saw only the squat farmhouse and endless rows of olive trees that she had seen before. There was a building behind the farmhouse that she assumed held what livestock the old man kept, but as she had heard no other noises that indicated the presence of animals, she thought it likely the farmer only kept the animals he intended to eat.

"Thatcher?" she said again, and now he turned toward her, not quite looking at her, but through her, as if wrestling a thought so complex in his mind, he required a point on which to fix to figure it all out. She shuffled from foot to foot, feeling ridiculously exposed in her bar wench costume while the dirty American sat in their rescuer's cart, seeming to ponder the meaning of life.

"Thatcher," she said once more, but this time with an edge that she had hoped she needn't use.

He moved then , standing up, his booted feet creating a billow of dust as they struck the hard dirt of the yard. And when he turned to her, she forced a smile in hopes to ease his mood, but he stopped her with, "We're leaving."

Her smile vanished.

* * *

A FARM.

His boots rested on farmland.

Again.

He looked up at the sky, his hand automatically moving to shield his eyes from the most intense rays, and in looking, his mind went to another sky, one of such brilliant blue he had stared at it in wonder for hours and hours until his mama called him from his roost in the open doors of the hay loft on the southern end of the barn.

But this wasn't that farm, and he most certainly wasn't in Carolina. This was Naples, Italy, and there was nothing friendly or whimsical about it. He dropped his hand and swung his gaze to his unlikely companion. He had seen her fall as she had gotten out of the carriage, and a gentleman would have sprung to help her up. But he hadn't been thinking just then . He had simply been feeling and reacting. Reacting to what, he did not want to say for in naming it, he would allow the memories to surface once more.

"We're leaving," he said again, but with more resolve now that his legs were solid beneath him.

The Countess of Stirling only blinked at him while their

rescuer remained in the same position, slightly hunched at the shoulders, gray, wiry hairy mussed from where he had scratched his head, hands fisted on his hips, his smashed hat in one of them. The man did not squint in the sun as much as Thatcher found himself doing, and for a moment, Thatcher thought of his father. The image was fleeting and fuzzy, and Thatcher did what was necessary to push the rest of it from his mind.

"We're going back to the port and finding the first ship bound for England."

"Thatcher, I must disagree with your conclusion," Kate said then , and his restless gaze finally came to rest on her.

In the current situation, it was probably the best place for him to look. The perfectly cultivated rows of olive trees, the menagerie of farm tools spread with seeming carelessness along the side of the barn beyond the squat farmhouse, and the chickens pecking at the ground only yards from his feet all served to make his uneasiness grow with an agility he was starting to fear.

But even as he noticed these things, he noticed a certain hint of neglect about the place. Having watched the practiced precision of his father attending to chores on the farm, Thatcher knew when something was not quite right. Like the band saw that lay perched against the side of the barn. There were some tools that could be left out in the elements but others that would rust if not put away properly. Or the milking stool with the broken leg tilted against the open barn door. And then the still full cart of olives that a single man was presumably taking to port for trade with the aid of a donkey and a nearly dilapidated cart that didn't seem right. His uneasiness grew.

Perhaps if he looked at the stunning Countess of Stirling, his racing thoughts would once more fall under his control, and this would be nothing more than an inconvenient stop on the much larger journey he had been on since the time he had left the last farm at sixteen. Perhaps luck would have it that history would replay itself and circumstances would find him leaving this farm under less than voluntary conditions.

"Disagree?" he said, and Kate shook her head.

"We cannot go back into port. They're looking for us."

Her reasoning was sound, but it did not mean Thatcher had to agree with it.

"Then what is your great plan, Countess? I don't suppose you're waiting for me to have another vision?"

He shifted his booted feet, scraping at the dirt. He needed to get out of this. The prison cell made him feel more comfortable than the sounds of horses and what might have been a cow coming from the barn.

Kate frowned, drawing her own fisted hands to her hips in a startlingly humorous imitation of their rescuer. And with this realization came another one. He still did not know who the mystery gentleman was.

"Excuse me," he said then , but his sentence went unfinished when a door slammed open somewhere and a call of "Luigi!" sounded across the yard.

Thatcher turned in the direction of the farmhouse just as a woman of equal size and shape to the edifice she had just exited emerged from the shadow of the eaves of the house, her hands working vigorously in the soft, faded apron tied at her plump waist. What she said after her tremendous proclamation of Luigi, Thatcher didn't know because the woman said it in Italian. He looked at Kate, but she watched the woman carefully, presumably listening to what the woman said to their mystery rescuer whom Thatcher now presumed was the Luigi the woman had proclaimed him to be.

The woman may have stopped her speech, but Thatcher could not hear a break in the woman's words, because suddenly Kate spoke. He stared at her, watching the way her mouth formed sounds he had never heard before. She had a beautiful voice, strong and clear, and it had the ability to mesmerize him when he least expected it. Like now when he stood on a farm for the first time in more than fifteen years, just the sound of her voice had his thoughts halting, freezing in the storm that swirled about his mind as if there were no reason for such pandemonium. And then Kate looked at him.

"She says we can stay," she said, her voice soft and, for the first time since he had met her, slightly unsure.

There was something in her tone that bothered him.

"Stay?" he said, and even the word itself felt brittle in his mouth.

"This is Rosa," Kate said then , indicating the rotund woman who had finally stopped trying to shred her apron into little bits with her bare hands. "And this is Luigi Salvatore." Here she indicated their mystery rescuer.

Thatcher nodded at each of them and would have taken off his hat in acknowledgement if he still had his hat. But as he didn't, he simply nodded in respect. Rosa threw up her hands at this, said something he didn't understand, and came toward him. Reaching up from her very low height, she grabbed his neck, drawing his head down. In quick secession, she placed a kiss on each of his cheeks, and then took his chin in her hand as she mumbled something that had Kate and Luigi smiling. From the bent position, he looked to Kate for translation.

"She says you look like her youngest son. She misses him," Kate said.

Thatcher tried to nod, but the woman still held his chin in her hand.

"Grazie," he murmured, hoping he pronounced the word correctly.

A smile instantly came to the folds of the woman's aged

face, and Thatcher, in turn, smiled as well. When she released him, he straightened, adjusting his jacket and shirt from where the material had shifted. The woman turned away from their group and started back toward the farmhouse, her hands in the air as she carried on a conversation that appeared to be largely one sided. Thatcher looked at Kate and Luigi to see if the woman expected a response, but as neither of them spoke until after the woman had disappeared into the house, Thatcher thought a response was not anticipated or desired.

Now Luigi stepped forward. "You come from England, then ?" he said, his English crisp but practiced, the cadence that of someone who has learned the language and had not been born speaking it.

Thatcher nodded. "Her ladyship, the Countess of Stirling, comes from England," he said, gesturing toward Kate. "Myself, I come from America. The Carolinas, specifically."

At this, Luigi's eyes widened, and he said, "America," as if the word were an uncomfortable shape in his mouth.

Thatcher smiled. "Yes, America," he said.

"You come inside and take food. You must be hungry," he said and with this he began to walk toward the door Rosa had just disappeared through.

"I think we should be returning to the port," Thatcher said, instead of following Luigi. "We need to get out of this place. No offense meant," he added, when he realized how it sounded. Naples was really a truly beautiful place. One of the most beautiful Thatcher had seen since he began his long, wandering journey, but it was full of people who wanted to imprison them or perhaps kill them, and neither option was appealing.

Luigi only stopped briefly.

"I'm afraid you cannot get out, American," he said and continued in the direction of the door.

Thatcher looked to Kate, but she was looking at Luigi now going through the same door that Rosa had used moments earlier. When she finally turned toward him, he saw the slump of her shoulders before he heard the sigh that left her lips.

"I believe we are stuck, Mr. Thatcher," she said.

He shook his head. "We're not stuck. We made it out of that prison cell, and we'll make it on a ship bound for England. We got here on a ship, we'll get out of here on a ship."

Kate shook her head, but Luigi was suddenly coming back through the door, a hunk of what appeared to be bread in each hand. Several stunted strides later, he plunked a chunk of bread in each of their hands, a smile spreading across his face. Thatcher looked at the bread, still warm from the oven, its center so porous and voluminous, he could almost picture sinking his teeth into it, and his stomach growled.

"You eat. You be happy. It will be all right," Luigi said and then moved past them.

Thatcher watched the little man go, walking over to the cart and beginning the task of unhitching the donkey from the front of the cart. Thatcher had watched his own father complete such a task many times before only then it had been a Clydesdale, a working horse of great stature that had pulled the plow through the fields and turned the earth of South Carolina until the fragrance of fresh soil rose in the air. Thatcher sniffed before he could remember where he was and that the robust soil of South Carolina did not lay under his feet. He shuffled his boots as if to confirm this fact, but it did little good. He was still in Naples, and he was still in danger.

He looked over at Kate and for the first time, realized how much more danger she was in. Katharine Cavanaugh, the Countess of Stirling, was a spy for England. A true, documented secret agent for the War Office. If she were caught, she would be tortured and killed. Thatcher, on the other hand, was a mercenary. He belonged to no country, and no country belonged to him. The War Office hired him to do jobs now and then , but if he were caught, his captors would think he could be bought. He couldn't, not by anyone in league with Napoleon, but his captors needn't know that. But Katharine. His mind flashed to another time when someone else had needed protecting, someone he had failed.

"We need to be going," he said again. But for some reason, his resolve weakened, and the words did not come out with the force he had intended.

The donkey made a noise as Luigi released the tethers, and the animal's head came up and about in protest. Luigi patted its nose and flank, mumbling to the animal.

"My oldest boy, Angelo, he had a better way with this animal than me. I cannot get him to do anything." Luigi turned to look at him, his full smile on his face once more. "This animal really is a – what is the word for it? – It is ass. Yes, he is ass."

Luigi smiled with such obvious joy, Thatcher couldn't help but smile in return even as he felt he was missing something very important. Kate had not said anything in several minutes, hardly at all in fact since Rosa had come and departed their company. He looked at her now as if his mere glance would get her to speak, but she did not.

"Angelo was good with all the animals. Now the cow does not like to give up her milk. She only give up her milk for Angelo." This statement was followed by several mumbled words in Italian, and then looking to the sky, the small Italian man crossed himself.

Kate still did not speak.

"Luigi, where are your sons?" Thatcher asked then , but

the suspicion he had been feeling all along had begun to creep up the back of his neck, making him shiver in the heat of the Mediterranean sun. Luigi released the donkey from the cart, walking the animal in the direction of the barn, but he stopped for a moment, turning back to Thatcher and Kate.

"Angelo, my oldest son, Paulo, my middle son, and Bruno, my youngest son, they are all gone," he said, and then Thatcher's stomach flipped over.

"Gone?" he asked.

Luigi nodded, gaining a better grip on the donkey's harness.

"They escape to Sicily before the general can make them a part of his army."

Thatcher waited, his breath steady in his lungs even as his heart began to race. "Escaped? When did they escape?"

Luigi settled his grip on the donkey's harness, and when he looked at Thatcher again, his smile had vanished.

"Three months now they've been gone. It's been three months since the general's men have searched every ship that leaves the port."

Thatcher looked at Kate, who only looked back at him, the expression on her face unreadable. He turned back to Luigi, but the man was already walking toward the barn, the donkey trailing reluctantly behind him. When Kate touched his arm, he jumped. She had moved so silently he hadn't expected to find her standing there beside him. But then she was, her eyes scanning his face, and for a moment, he felt vulnerable and unsure. No one had studied him with such scrutiny in a very long time, and certainly, no woman had been tall enough to look him in the eye the way she did. It left him uneasy at the same time that he enjoyed it.

"We're stuck, I reckon," he said, and Kate nodded.

"I reckon," she said.

CHAPTER 3

"We'll go by land then," Thatcher said as he reclined in his chair at the Salvatores' kitchen table a few hours later.

They had taken the time to wash some of the dirt off their arms and face using water from the well in the front yard before making their way into the farmhouse. The extensive, and thoroughly decadent, meal that Rosa had laid out for them now lay in ruins across the table's surface. Kate had watched Rosa make the sheets for the lasagna, mixing egg into the dough and rolling the sheets with exquisite precision. The small woman was efficient in the kitchen, babbling on about this year's tomato crop and the unnecessary lack of zucchini. She seemed rather perturbed about the abundant lack of zucchini, and Kate wondered what magic the woman worked with the vegetable.

And the tomatoes, picked fresh from the garden, had oozed flavor, and Kate had wanted to try them even before they made their way into the sauce. The aroma of baking sausage had her bending over the stove, as if by getting closer the smell would permeate her very skin and fill her with the essence of the browning meat. It was true, her obvious delight in the meal bordered on ridiculous, but she didn't care. Surviving on hard sea biscuits for days as they had made their way across the water to Naples had been one of the lowest points of her life, and the myriad smells and sights of Rosa Salvatore's kitchen had been an oasis of carnal pleasure. And Kate had taken the liberty of basking in it.

Now she sopped up the last of the sauce on her plate with the soft, yeasty bread that Rosa made fresh in her stone oven, pushing the entire thing into her mouth in one savory bite. She looked up at Thatcher's statement only to find him staring at her.

"You really like food, don't you?" he said.

She nodded, feeling no shame at all in the observation. She did like food, and at nearly six feet tall, she liked a lot of food, probably more than what was deemed appropriate for a young lady. But Kate did not really care. Her mother had never said anything about her eating habits, nor had she fashioned any rules around what Kate should or should not eat. So Kate ate.

"Do you think it's wise to leave a territory occupied by a tyrant's brother-in-law to enter the territory occupied by said tyrant?" Kate asked, getting them back onto the matter at hand.

Thatcher didn't make an outward indication that he had heard her. He looked rather steeped in his own thoughts. She picked up her glass of wine, swirling the colorful liquid before taking a sip. The wine was pungent with vibrant fruit tones and whispers of lavender. She enjoyed the slide of it down her throat and the resulting burst of heat in her stomach. She reached for the bottle to refill Thatcher's glass and her own when Thatcher suddenly sat up.

"How did the Salvatore sons get out of Naples?" Thatcher asked.

Kate set down his glass, now topped off with wine. "Like Luigi said, they got out before Murat's men started searching the ships for anyone trying to leave without permission."

"But how does one get permission?" he asked, and for a moment, he looked like a child who had just been given a present.

She paused for a moment, enjoying the sight. But just as quickly she shook her head as if to dislodge the ridiculous notion, forcing her mind to focus on the task at hand. Their mission may have been botched, but she was still a spy for the War Office.

"I do not know how one gets permission. But I'll wager that it involves having a lot of money, which we don't. We must think of another way out."

The door in the rear of the kitchen opened then , ending their conversation. Kate felt a spike of frustration at being interrupted. But Luigi ambled in, carrying a crate of some kind overflowing with green, leafy vegetables, and curiosity at what those vegetables were to be used for overrode any frustration at having their strategy session abruptly ended. Luigi spoke with someone behind him, and soon Rosa emerged, carrying a bowl filled with potatoes. They finished their conversation just as Rosa made her way to the table, depositing the bowl on its surface.

"She's very happy to have people to feed," Luigi said, coming up to the table and drawing a chair out to sit.

His body seemed to fold into the chair, his short legs collapsing beneath him, and for the first time, Kate realized how old the man was. He must have been older than his sixtieth year, and yet, he tended an entire olive farm.

"Luigi, how old are your sons?" she asked in English so Thatcher could understand.

Rosa had gone over to the oven to check on another batch of bread she was baking, and Luigi followed her with his eyes.

"Angelo, he is my first son, and he was born forty-four years ago. Paulo came next, forty-two years ago. And then the baby. Baby Bruno. He came forty years ago."

Kate felt her eyes go wide.

"So your sons must have families of their own," Thatcher said, leaning on the table as he picked up his glass of wine.

Luigi's face broke into the smile Kate had come to expect from it.

"Big families!" he cried, spreading his hands as far apart as he could reach.

His pronouncement brought Rosa to the table, her hands wrinkled in the fabric of her apron in concern, but Luigi quickly explained what Thatcher had asked and soon the woman smiled, too.

Rosa broke into a quick history of the boys and their families. There was Angelo and Maria and the six babies. There was Paulo and Adelina and the four babies. And there was baby Bruno and Doretea and the three babies, but God bless the souls of all the babies they had lost. Rosa crossed herself and hurried back to the oven.

"The babies aren't really babies, are they, Luigi?" Kate asked then , and Thatcher looked quickly at her. He obviously had not understood what Rosa had said, but Kate hoped to get more information before she explained to Thatcher.

Luigi shook his head. "The youngest is sixteen years of age. They are no longer babies, but thinking of them as such, makes Rosa a happy woman," he said.

Kate relayed this information to Thatcher, who then turned to Luigi.

"They all helped you on the farm, didn't they?"

Luigi cocked his head at this as if puzzled. "Helped? This word does not seem right. They all worked the farm. This land belongs to them. There is no helping."

"So you have been without all of them for three months?" Kate asked then , and Luigi nodded in the positive.

Thatcher made a noise of understanding then and sat back in his seat as if something had suddenly become clear to him. Kate didn't know what that was, but he seemed satisfied with himself for the first time since coming to the Salvatore's farm.

"How did they all leave?" Kate asked then , hoping they might glean some more information that would help them get out of Naples.

Luigi pushed through the remaining platters of food on the table as if inspecting that they had eaten enough.

"We were able to pay for passage for the families, each of them, before the soldiers started checking the boats. But then it was too late for Rosa and me. We did not make it," he said.

Thatcher leaned forward again, his elbows resting on the edge of the table as he steepled his fingers. "What do you mean too late?"

Kate recognized Thatcher's attempt at extracting more detailed information and admired his skill as an interrogator. They knew one needed permission to leave Naples, but they would need more than that to understand how they would eventually escape the country.

"Each passenger needs to have papers to leave the country. The general demanded it. Rosa and I did not have permission, and it was not granted to us."

"The general?" Kate asked, remembering that Luigi had used that term when they had unloaded from the cart earlier.

Luigi nodded, picking up a piece of the bread from the

table. "The general manages things here in Naples for Murat. He rules from the building you two came out of earlier today."

Kate thought back to the officer they had been brought before earlier that morning upon arriving in Naples and wondered if that was the general of which Luigi spoke.

Thatcher must have drawn the same conclusion because he asked, "The general wears a fancy uniform and likes to give orders?"

Luigi nodded as his mouth was now full of bread.

"You must be able to buy permission," Thatcher said then , and Luigi's eyes grew round.

"Yes, American, yes, you can, but it is precious," Luigi said around the bread in his mouth.

"Precious?" Thatcher asked, looking to her instead of Luigi.

She asked Luigi in Italian to clarify, and Luigi told her it required a lot of money to buy permission, money that the Salvatores did not have as they had taken their entire savings to get their children and their children's families out of Naples. She relayed this to Thatcher, and they sat then in silence, letting this information sink in.

And then Luigi sat up. "You come with money?" he asked.

Thatcher looked at Kate, and she knew he was silently questioning how much to tell this man who had been unknown to them only hours before. Only now they sat around his scarred wooden kitchen table having eaten a feast that would have pleased monarchs, Kate was sure. And for that hospitality how much did they owe him? A spy never gave away information that would not gain her something in return, but in their current situation, that didn't sit right with Kate.

Thatcher seemed to read her thoughts, because he leaned

closer to Luigi and said, "We do not want to put you and your wife in danger. You gave us aid when we most needed it, and for that, we are grateful. I will tell you why we are here in Naples, and you can decide whether or not you wish us to stay."

Thatcher paused then , and Kate looked to Luigi who had not moved or made a sound. The bread he had been chewing was long gone, and his face relaxed into the folds it had grown accustomed to. His eyes remained fuzzy in the dim light of the kitchen as the light from the door and the room's single window above the dry sink did not penetrate far into the room. Kate waited, feeling the pace of her heart rate pick up. A spy never revealed her identity no matter the cost. But Kate had never encountered a cost quite so high as the one she faced now. Thatcher continued.

"Katharine Cavanaugh, the Countess of Stirling, is a spy for the British War Office. Myself, I'm a hired mercenary. I carry out work for the highest bidder when assigned. In this particular instance, it's the British War Office as well."

Luigi still did not move.

Thatcher continued, "We were on an assignment to rescue a colleague who had been kidnapped and was likely being traded to the French. We were pursued, and we escaped by boarding a ship in the port of Dover. Our only mistake was in not knowing where the ship was bound. We hid amongst the cargo, stealing food and water as we could, for the duration of the voyage. Upon arriving in Naples, we were taken into custody when we tried to exit the ship."

Having finished, Thatcher spread his hands as if to say that was all and sat back in the chair.

"You do not come with money then ," Luigi finally said, and it was as if a door had suddenly been opened and a gale of fresh air swept through the room.

Kate looked at Thatcher. A smile tugged at the corner of his mouth, but beyond that, Thatcher made no motion, until slowly one hand dipped beneath the table, and Kate saw him digging in the pocket of his ruined trousers for something. He finally pulled his hand free and dropped several coins on the table.

"We have that," Thatcher said.

"That will not buy you freedom," Luigi said, his fuzzy eyes moving over the coins. "That will not even buy you a loaf of bread."

A snicker escaped Kate's lips before she could stop it, and the sound emerged as something of a snort. A hand automatically came up to cover her face as if to unconsciously hide the social misstep, but Luigi only smiled at her.

"It is fun, is it not?" he said, and then with a triumphant push on his thighs he stood up, all five foot six inches of him. "We do something else then ," he said and moved in the direction of the back door.

Thatcher stood now, his body suddenly so tense, Kate could see the change from across the table. "What is it we're going to do?"

Kate's mind raced with the same question and all possible answers as she watched the little Italian move toward the door of his home after Thatcher had just revealed their biggest secret, a secret that could possibly bring Luigi the money he needed for him and his wife to reunite with their family in Sicily. Kate's breath froze in her lungs and a peculiar chill creeped down her spine. The room had grown impossibly cold or perhaps it was just her.

In all of her missions she had never felt such peril. She had always been removed from it, a veneer standing between her and the action about her. The action in which the great Katharine Cavanaugh, the Countess of Stirling, took center stage but always bowed out before the curtain fell. But now

Thatcher stood beside her, almost literally. She could not control the parts of the other players and how well they played their roles. She could only take care of her own part, and suddenly, that was not enough. But she didn't know why.

"For now," Luigi said, turning slightly toward them as he pulled his cap back on his head, "We do chores," he finished, his face folded into the now familiar smile.

"Chores?" Kate said about as gracefully as her earlier snort had been.

Luigi's smile slid dramatically from his face, his expression falling into that of mock confusion. "This is a farm, is it not?"

Kate nodded.

"Then we do chores," he said and went out through the door.

* * *

Thatcher didn't move right away.

He had heard what the old man had said, his voice thick with the tones of his native tongue, but in his mind, it was another voice that he had heard, a sterner voice, one drawled more than spoken. And for a moment, Thatcher stood beneath the giant oak that acted as sentry to the front porch of their home in the ridges of Carolina, and for a moment, his father stood in front of him, calling him and his brother to chores, and for just a moment, Thatcher remembered Thomas' face. The joy in it when being called to help on the farm. There was such promise in that face. Promise he had selfishly left unprotected.

But then he blinked, and he was standing in a rustic kitchen again, the dim light of not enough windows and doors forcing his eyes to strain into the darkness to make out shapes and objects. He turned his head, but the countess had not moved from her chair. She remained seated, her back so straight he thought he could use it to plane boards. He sat back down in the chair he had just vacated and let his head drop back, his dirty hair sliding along his forehead until it covered his eyes.

He smelled. Bad. And he was sure he looked even worse. Doing chores wouldn't make a lick of difference to his state of hygiene, so he might as well get up and go help the man who had rescued them. His mind drifted for a moment to the rather convenient arrival of Mr. Luigi Salvatore, but it only lingered there for a moment. There was nothing about Luigi that would alert Thatcher to any possible motives behind the man's deed except sheer understanding. His own family had fled the very people that had taken over their beloved Naples. Why wouldn't he help a stranger threatened by the very same people?

But how had Luigi even known that?

"Do you think he loiters about the prison rescuing strangers on a daily basis?"

Thatcher picked up his head, blinking at the uncanny ability of Katharine Cavanaugh to read his mind.

"I was wondering the same myself," he said and fully straightened, reaching across the table for the bottle of wine Rosa had left out for them. He spun the bottle around in his fingers, the light playing off the tones of glass.

"It concerns me a bit that a gentleman of his advanced years and obviously deficient funds would so willingly harbor the enemy."

Thatcher felt one of his eyebrows go up. "You mean you think he's going to sell us to the highest bidder?"

Kate shrugged, the motion doing wonderful things to her generous bosom. "Perhaps. He has obvious use for the money."

Thatcher was already shaking his head. "It doesn't fit," he said.

Kate took a sip from her wine glass but carefully replaced it on the table, her fingers playing carelessly with the stem.

"No, it doesn't, does it?" she said, but there was something about her tone that told him she didn't expect a response from him.

So he sat in the dim light of Rosa Salvatore's kitchen and admired Katharine Cavanaugh. He had worked with several members of the aristocracy, and titles had long since lost the flash that they held for the regular American who craved the mystique of a monarchy they did not wish to rule them. The Countess of Stirling was just Katharine Cavanaugh, or Kate rather, and he liked that just fine.

Kate was turning out to be a bit of a strange girl. She was tall, for starters, and not a willow slip of a girl. She was, in fact, all very much woman, from her broad shoulders to her ample bosom to her long stride. She could keep pace with him and not complain that he was moving too quickly. When he looked at her, he didn't strain his neck trying to tilt his head down far enough to look her in the eye.

And she ate.

Katharine Cavanaugh ate a lot, and she apparently liked it very much. She wasn't fat though or even the slightest bit plump. If anything, Kate was sturdy. That was the word for her. She was a sturdy woman. It was a description his mother would have used on her.

"So are we trusting him then ? Luigi and Rosa Salvatore of Naples?"

Thatcher heard the degree of reluctance in her voice.

"What about the situation bothers you? Except everything," he said.

Kate picked up her glass once more as her eyes stared at

something above his head, her mind obviously on the thoughts plaguing her conscience.

"It seems too easy that he should just appear at the exact moment we needed him," she said.

"Agreed," Thatcher responded, but he could tell she had more to say and waited.

"I'm concerned our position here is exposing them to undue danger."

"It likely is, but the separation from their sons and their sons' family is probably a driving force behind their decision to harbor us. Protecting an enemy of the state doesn't come lightly, but neither does sending off your children to save their very lives."

Kate looked at him now, drawing her gaze down from the clouds of her mind to look at him. "I don't follow," she said.

"I beg your pardon," Thatcher said.

Kate leaned forward then , her face moving into the light so he could better read her features.

"Why would the separation from their sons drive them to do something so dangerous?"

Thatcher shrugged. "It's a terrible decision they had to make. Separating themselves from their own children and grandchildren just to ensure their safety. I can't imagine what that must have been like, but I'll reckon if they can do anything to get back at the people that caused them to make such a decision, then they'd like the chance to do it."

Kate only blinked at him.

"Wouldn't you do anything you could to protect your family?"

Kate shook her head. "I'm not sure I have the same understanding of family that you do, Thatcher," she finally said.

"What do you mean?" he asked.

He didn't know much about Kate Cavanaugh, but she

must have a father and mother somewhere that would help her relate to what he was saying.

"Well, wouldn't you feel the need to get back at the person who separated you from your children? I mean, when you have them some day."

Kate frowned. "I have never thought about such a topic, Mr. Thatcher. My direction has always been with the War Office. A family is not something that goes along with that."

Now it was Thatcher's turn to frown. "How long have you worked for the War Office?" Thatcher said then , studying Kate features. She didn't appear to be more than twenty-seven or twenty-eight years of age, but he could be wrong about her. She carried herself with the poise of someone a great deal older.

"Ten years," she said.

"And how old are you?"

"Eight and twenty, but why is that relevant?" she responded quickly.

Thatcher sat up suddenly. "Ten years and you're eight and twenty?"

She nodded.

"You began working for the War Office immediately upon entering society?"

Kate shrugged. "It was expected of me," she said.

Thatcher raised both eyebrows then , the pieces of the puzzle that was Kate Cavanaugh coming together to form a picture he did not like.

"How is it that working for the War Office is expected? Especially for a woman. No offense intended. It's just that I've always been raised to treat women as the ladies they are with the respect and honor owed to a person who has the strength to be a mother."

Kate tilted her head as if he were extremely daft. "I'm not sure what my sex and its history as caregivers has to do with the matter, but my father is Captain Edward Hadley," she said then , but Thatcher only continued to hold his eyebrows up. "Oh, you're not English, are you then ?" she said, her face breaking into a smile that stretched across her rather squarish face. "Captain Hadley, my father, is a second son, you see, of the Earl of Bainbridge, so as a second son, he was commissioned in the Navy but was utter rubbish at it. He had a talent for the law though, which was rather unnatural for the son of an earl, but he was a second son after all. He was removed from active duty, read the law at Cambridge, and stationed in the War Office. He's top counsel or something there now. Everyone knows Captain Hadley."

She shrugged, her brown hair swishing about her face as if to emphasize the naturalness of it all.

"Captain Hadley," Thatcher repeated, not understanding at all how that was supposed to help him to understand things.

Kate sighed, apparently reading his expression. "Thatcher, my father had no sons. It's up to me to carry out his legacy as an honorable agent for the War Office. As such, I have dedicated myself to my position as an agent. It has left no room for such frivolous thoughts as marriage and a family."

He watched her face as she spoke, noting the way she didn't quite meet his eyes as if there was something about her statement that bothered her. He didn't push her though as they had more pressing matters to discuss.

"Well, daughter of the Captain Hadley, I suppose it's time for you to show off your skills as an agent of the War Office. You are stranded behind enemy lines, in a presumably hostile situation. You have taken refuge with a sympathizer. What are your next moves?"

Kate cocked her head. "My instinct tells me to gather further information."

"You mean spy," Thatcher said.

Kate nodded. "But what information am I trying to gather?" She leaned forward then , placing her elbow on the table to rest her chin in her hand. She had a dimple in her chin, just a small indentation and for some strange reason, he wanted to place his finger just there to see what it felt like. He imagined the warmth of her skin, the softness of it. He swallowed.

"What are our objectives?"

"Retreat," Kate said, but she stopped her own word. "No, not retreat. We have nothing to retreat from. We must retrace our steps."

The light coming through the lone window in the room shot gold strands through her brown hair, and Thatcher found it terribly distracting. How could such a woman never have thought of marriage? The thought saddened him.

"Take advantage of the situation?" Thatcher supplied, forcing his mind back to the matter of espionage.

Kate nodded. "We need to find out where Murat's forces are and where they are planning to be next," she said, sitting up straight, her face a study in triumph.

"And do what with that information? We're stuck in Italy."

He hated to say the words, but there was something about debating with this woman that gave him a little flash of pleasure he had not felt in some time. He perversely wanted to prolong it.

"Good point, Mr. Thatcher," she said, sitting back in her chair and crossing her own arms under her bosom. Her lack of intact clothing was emphasized with such a move, but he tried not to notice.

"I still think we should find out where Murat's forces are and what their next plans might be," she said, once again looking at a space above his head. "But we need to get out of the country or the information is useless."

"And we can't buy our way out because we have no money."

"Can we smuggle ourselves out like we smuggled ourselves in?" she asked.

Thatcher thought about it a moment but shook his head. "Unlikely. They'll be sure to be watching for us now."

She nodded and continued to stare at the space above his head until she suddenly sat up, leaning so far forward on the table now that he knew he could reach out that finger and touch the indent at her chin. She was so close he saw the specks of green in her hazel eyes, flecks of color in a sea of warm brown. And she was excited.

"You're right!" she said, her voice emphatic but restrained as if practiced in the art of controlled elation. "We do go by land."

"How do you figure?" He leaned forward, his crossed arms resting on the table top, leaning as close as he dared to her, their breaths mingling, the pungent scent of wine strong between them.

"Napoleon has just escaped Elba. He's on a rampage across Europe. He's left his brother-in-law to take care of a meager conquered country like the Kingdom of Naples. Murat--"

"Must be feeling slighted," Thatcher picked up the story.

"As any gentleman would, he finds himself yearning to prove his brother-in-law mistaken," Kate continued.

"He's going to do something stupid," Thatcher inserted, drawing another snorted laugh from Kate. The sound was rather indelicate, and he could understand why, every time she emitted the noise, she tried to hide behind her hand, but this time, he was close enough to catch her hand, draw it away from her face.

"You shouldn't hide like that," he said, his voice unexpectedly soft, "Especially when you're laughing."

Her skin was warm, the pads of her fingertips softly callused, a tantalizing roughness he hadn't expected on the hands of a lady. He held her hand, unable to let go. But she let him hold it, so he didn't bother to force himself to release it. And they stared at each other.

Thatcher had been with enough women to know when one sought his attention, but he had never been with a woman who outwardly stared at him. Especially not a countess who stared at him with such heat burning in her eyes. And if he were right about it, unknown heat. He wanted to ask her what she was thinking, what she was feeling. But all he could do was look at her, hold her hand, while he stared at her and wondered.

What the hell had he gotten himself into?

He lusted after a woman who had never even thought of marriage. Normally, such a situation would intrigue him, fit naturally into his own chosen lifestyle of zero connections, but with Kate, it didn't sit right.

But the struggling thoughts only lingered in his mind for a second, because then she kissed him.

It was so unexpected he didn't respond at first. Her lips met his at an awkward angle as she strained across the table to close the small gap that remained between them. But her lips were lush and full, her wide mouth caressing. He surged forward, as far as the table would allow him, pressing into the kiss, until suddenly she was gone again.

She stood abruptly, knocking her chair back and to the floor. The sound was like the branch of a tree snapping in a thunderstorm. He reflexively grabbed his head as if to hold onto his hat, only his hat was still gone, lost somewhere between Dover and Naples. He stood though, his body a mix of confused feelings and emotions. Kate stared at him, her eyes wide and wondering.

"I don't know why I did that," she said then , her breath a rush of air, her words slurred in their haste.

He didn't say anything, likely because he didn't know what to say. Kate backed away from the table, and he knew he needed to speak, but nothing would come. Until she said, "I really should find some clothes to put on," and turned to hurry from the room, knocking over another chair in her progress.

And still he said nothing.

CHAPTER 4

*K*ate stared at the horse stall and imagined a grand bed in its place. Mahogany four poster so high it required a step to enter it with a mattress perfectly feathered from only the best down and pillows so plump they swallowed one's head upon lying down. The bed in her mind was a far sight better than the straw contraption sitting before her with its obvious bare spots that showed the ground beneath it. But Luigi had worked hard to put together something close to being hospitable, and Kate was determined to appreciate it.

"Damn you, Thatcher," she muttered under her breath as she tested the bed with a gentle prod of her foot.

"What was that, little lady?"

She jumped when Thatcher's voice sounded so close to her ear. Putting her foot back on solid ground, she swung around to find him standing so close to her, she could see the wet spots on his shirt from where his freshly washed hair had dampened the fabric. Seeing the wet spots on the fabric reminded her of her rather indelicate situation as a result of her own bath. Rosa may have had a gown for her to borrow, but the woman had not had adequate undergarments. So Kate stood there before Thatcher feeling the rush of the cold night air between her exposed thighs as her under things hung on the line outside, drying in the wind.

Her stomach rolled with not only the thought that she was inadequately dressed but at the sight of the very thing that had so upset her carefully laid plans in recent days. She had not seen him since that terrible encounter in the kitchen earlier that day when she had acted like an utter fool. She closed her eyes briefly and focused her mind.

It didn't matter that his tight fitting trousers perfectly accentuated the muscles of his thighs or that the shirt tucked into his breeches showed off his narrow hips and flat stomach or that his carelessly tossed curled hair begged her to run her fingers through it. Kate snapped her eyes open, focusing on the confusion that swamped her at the mere sight of him. She was an agent for the War Office, and she did not have time for such silly nonsense as physical attraction to a man and what that may mean. With resolve, the confusion faded, and she was once again in control of herself.

"I don't see why it's necessary for us to sleep in the barn," she said then .

Thatcher smiled his wicked smile at her. "I don't believe that is what you said, but I'll amuse you. We've already put Luigi and Rosa in enough danger just by being here. Should anyone come looking for us in the night, it will be better if we're sleeping in the barn. It'll look like we snuck in and took up residence without the Salvatores knowing."

Kate could not find fault in his logic and only nodded in response. "Well, good night, Thatcher," she said and made her way into her stall. She didn't bother to look behind her to see what Thatcher was doing, but soon, she heard noises that sounded as if he, too, were settling in for the night.

She pulled aside the voluminous folds of her borrowed gown, unearthing one booted foot to once again poke at the straw bed. The gown she wore was simple and dated, its original owner much wider than Kate, and a good deal shorter. The garment, though ill fitting, did manage to cover the necessary areas, and Kate was confident with some alteration the next day, it might fit well. It was fortunate for Kate that Rosa had a rather robust daughter-in-law, or Kate would have had an entirely different predicament than the one she was in. She had several unnecessary visions of attempting to fit into one of the petite Rosa's gowns. They all did not end well.

Finding the straw bed to be adequate, she turned about to set herself into it. Once again, the borrowed gown proved to be rather cumbersome, but with some maneuvering, she made her way into the depths of the straw. And it felt glorious. For one, it did not smell like urine, feces, or other bodily functions. It did not rock consistently back and forth. And it was not accompanied by the sporadic sound of scurrying rats. It was soft with just a bit of firmness, fresh and airy, and as of yet, there was no rat accompaniment. Kate closed her eyes, absorbing the softness into her bones as her aching muscles relaxed for the first time in days.

As she lay there, enjoying the feeling of the silent dark surrounding her, the tent-like gown swallowing her in its embrace, for the first time in days, Kate realized how tired she was. It had been over a week since their accidental departure from Dover, and it had been a week of fitful rest and stolen moments of sleep in dangerous places. The Salvatores' barn was the closest thing she'd seen to safety in a very long time. And she was determined to enjoy it.

But even as her mind relaxed, her body did not. Visions of Thatcher flooded her mind, and she opened her eyes as if to escape the thoughts. He had no business invading her thoughts like that. There was only room in there for analyzing their current predicament and evaluating the necessary actions to remedy it.

But then why did she see him as he sat at the supper table across from her, his face washed, his hands cleaned, but the skin of his face unshaven, the light stubble of hair there beckoning in its temptation. She had wanted to reach out, run her fingers along his jaw to feel the scrape of it against her skin. She had never had such a thought in her entire life, and the very fact that she was having it now startled her. She reminded herself over and over again that she was an agent for the War Office, but it no longer held the resolve that it once did.

She sighed quietly and closed her eyes again.

In a matter of days she would be rid of the man and his unwanted appeal. She had only to persevere for a few days more, she was sure of it.

But then she became aware of fitful shuffling, the tossing and turning of a body unable to rest. She cataloged her own sense of relaxation against the billows of straw as it was her mind that made her unable to rest. For a perverse moment, she wanted to smile because she thought he deserved a bit of irritation as well. But then she blinked her eyes and frowned. It honestly pained her to hear Thatcher act so restlessly. She bit her lip, hoping he would settle, but he did not.

So finally, she said, "Thatcher?"

At first there was no response, only the scratchy sound of what might have been breathing coming from the stall next to hers. She listened, imagining for a moment that she would soon hear rats scurrying about once more, but when more silence came, she said again, "Thatcher?"

This time there was a reply. It wasn't so much as a word but a noise, sounding a lot like Mmmm. Kate wasn't sure if that meant she had been acknowledged, and she could keep talking or if she should be quiet, ignore him, and go to sleep. She liked that second bit a great deal more than the first and hoped she needn't say more. Turning onto her side and falling into a very, very deep sleep seemed ideal just then .

But then Thatcher started talking.

"You never finished telling me your idea," he said, and Kate blinked at the rafters of the hay loft above her head.

She could just make out the crisscrossing of beams in the moonlight that trickled through the slats of the barn, and she concentrated on connecting their forms until she could figure out of what he spoke.

"Murat," she finally said, remembering with too much clarity the conversation they had been having right before she had kissed him.

"It had sounded like you were onto something important. I'd like to hear the rest of it."

His words were normal enough, but the tone of his voice seemed off. It was overly controlled, brittle and terse. She twisted her head as if she could see him through the wooden wall that separated them. Obviously, she could not, but staring in his direction gave her a false sense of relief.

"I think Murat will try to take Italy. All of it."

She heard some movement in the stall next to hers, but Thatcher didn't say anything at first. She waited, her breathing the only sound she could hear.

"And if he does?"

She licked her lips, suddenly unsure of the plan that she had formulated in her head that had seemed so simple. Its simplicity suddenly seemed like a terrible thing, something that any green spy would recognize as a trap. But surely it wasn't.

"And then at the moment of greatest confusion, we escape," she said and having laid out her plan, suddenly felt her resolve harden for the first time in days.

* * *

HE HAD BEEN sixteen when he had left his father's farm in Carolina. Sixteen had seemed really old then . He was master of his universe, and nothing could get in his way. Or at least that was what he had said to himself then . And yet now, sixteen years later, he could remember the smell of fresh straw, and not because he currently found himself surrounded by it. It was something so engrained in his person that it would likely never be eradicated. No matter how hard he tried.

"We escape in the chaos?" he said then , pushing back the memories. "How?"

He hadn't liked how she had fled from him earlier that day. A mere brush of lips, and she had vanished on him. What had she said right before though? She hadn't meant to do that? Well, it had damn well felt like she had meant to do it. Her taste had been vibrant with the rich, earthy tones of the wine and bread from their meal. He had been starved for a woman's touch, but he didn't realize how much until that moment. But even as that realization came, another one came swiftly behind it. It was likely that not just any woman's touch would do. He very much feared that only Kate would do.

And this terrified him. Had she truly grown to be that important to him? He shook his head as if to push the thought from his mind. He couldn't be responsible for her. He just couldn't be, and if she were that important, then it was only a matter of time before he was responsible.

He heard a rustling in the straw on the other side of the wooden stall.

"A military maneuver is likely to create a certain level of chaos. Natives will begin to panic as their homeland is ravaged. Escape is likely to be a priority."

"We escape with the natives?" he interjected.

"Precisely. Over land. We can go across France and into Le Havre. We have a man stationed there who can get us across the Channel."

She made it sound so simple and easy. Just a little jaunt across the hostile territory of France, under the regime of one of the craziest, most ruthless bastards Thatcher had ever seen, and hop a ship to England. Sounded perfect.

"How do we get into France? What method of travel?"

There was a pause on the other side of the stall.

"I haven't thought that far through," came the reply.

He nodded even though Kate couldn't see him.

He thought for a moment that he should be more concerned than he was at that moment. It wasn't as if he had planned to end up behind enemy lines, and he most certainly had not planned to end up there with Kate, a woman who drove his senses perilously out of control. But he had been in odder situations, and he was certain he would be in odder ones yet. He just had to keep moving ahead, focusing on the things that would save them in the end.

And prevent Katharine Cavanaugh from becoming too important to him.

"I think we should ask Luigi for help," he finally said.

"Luigi?"

He thought he heard her pause to lick her lips, and even though he could not be certain of it as he could not see her, his stomach tightened nonetheless, imagining what it looked like.

"What kind of help?"

"Luigi knew enough to get his family out of the country before Murat and his men arrived. I think he knows people. Or at least knows allegiances. We can ask him what we should do."

He heard more rustling as if she were shaking her head

against the straw of her bed. He wondered suddenly if hers was as comfortable as his. Perhaps she'd let him test it out. He pushed the thought away as soon as it entered his mind. He had no right taking advantage of the situation, especially as it stood. Kate was as vulnerable as he was, if not more, in this situation. Although, he was fairly certain he would let her take advantage of him. A woman who had not even thought of marriage in her twenty-eight years would seem the perfect fit for him. Only nothing could be further from the truth, and his stomach clenched on the thought.

"I think it's too risky. Standard operating procedure dictates that we--"

"What did you wish to be when you grew up?" he cut her off before she could launch into a speech about spy etiquette.

He listened in the darkness waiting for her reply, but there was only silence next to him until he heard a clearly drawn in breath.

"I beg your pardon?"

"When you were a young girl, did you imagine yourself as an agent for the War Office of England? I mean, before you were told about the expectations your father had for you?"

More silence.

"Because you seem to be very good at following their directives, and I wondered how much time you've been studying their – what did you call it? – standard operating procedures?"

Even more silence.

He thought perhaps he had confused her with his interruption, but she made no move to clarify his statement so he waited. He heard her adjust a time or two as the straw rustled, and then her voice came, softer now, not as defined, mimicking what little light drifted through the plank boards of the barn walls.

"I do not think I understand your meaning," she said.

He smiled even though he could not see her. "Come now, little lady, surely, you had occasion to think about what it was you were going to do when you were older? Every little girl dreams of fairy tales coming true. Tell me, who was your Prince Charming?"

He knew he made his American accent rather thick there at the end, but it usually did the trick when trying to get a creature of the female persuasion to really talk to him. If he was going to get Katharine Cavanaugh to trust him enough to break free of the War Office's standard operating procedures, he had to get her talking. And honest talk. None of this dictating rules jargon. For some reason, he knew there was a Kate inside of her that had not always been so devoted to the War Office, who had had other dreams in her life, and he wanted to draw her out. He didn't know why. Such a maneuver would only serve to exacerbate the current tension between them, but more importantly, he had to know.

"Fairy tales, Thatcher?" she said then , and the pitch of confusion in her voice rang with such honesty that Thatcher felt his own confusion at his actions rising.

"Fairy tales," he said again. "What's your favorite?"

He knew as soon as the question left his mouth that he was not going to enjoy her answer. It was a flippant question meant to get her talking about herself, but he had a nagging suspicion that what he had asked was a dangerous question for Kate.

"I didn't read fairy tales when I was young," she said, and Thatcher's suspicions turned to regret.

"I'm sorry to hear that," he said. "What was it you did read?"

"Sophocles," she said, and Thatcher scratched his head. "In the original Greek." And Thatcher rolled his eyes.

"Sophocles?" he said, an image of a young Kate, brown

hair in pig tails, dressed in one of those little dresses with the smocks and buttoned up black boots, with a tome of Greek literature spread across her lap, so thick her legs likely went numb on occasion. "What about "The Little Glass Slipper"?" He had dug deep for that one, trying to remember what his little cousins had always been prattling on about when they were young.

""Cinderella?"" came the response through the wall.

"I reckon that's a strong enough female character for your pursuit," he said.

"I wasn't allowed to read fairy tales. It was not expected of me."

He turned toward the wall then as if he could suddenly see through the wood. "You weren't expected--"

He didn't finish the thought. The damn wall was getting in his way, and he didn't care for it. He pushed out of his straw bed and carefully made his way through the darkened barn to the other stall.

* * *

KATE HEARD HIM GET UP. She heard his footfalls on the dirt floor of the barn, heard him round the corner of the stalls. She sat up, her heart racing in her chest like a stampede of frightened sheep. She clutched at the billowing gown, pulling it against her body as if to protect her more acutely from the utter lack of undergarments.

And then he was there, standing in the open door of the stall, the filtered light splashing across his wide shoulders, narrow hips and long, long, long legs like some kind of great masterpiece, painted in oils and put up on the wall of some museum for people to gawk at. She would happily be one of those people.

"What are you doing?" she said, her voice ridiculously high for an equally ridiculous question.

"What do you mean reading fairy tales wasn't expected of you?"

He lounged in the doorway then , one elbow propped on the top of the stall, his hips leaning with just enough angle to emphasize, well, everything. She wanted to stare. She wanted to look away. She wanted there to be more light so she could see him properly.

"It wasn't expected of me. My mother--" She paused, licking her suddenly very dry lips. "My mother prepared me for what I was destined to become, and reading fairy tales was not part of the curriculum."

"Destined? What on God's green earth are talking about?" he said, and then he was moving.

He stepped into the stall, remnants of straw crackling under his boots. She wanted to back up. She wanted to run away. She wanted to sit in his lap. And when he sat down in the straw next to her, she almost squeaked, pulling the folds of her dress out of the way of his descending body.

"I beg your pardon," she said, because right then it was the only thing she could say.

She had never been stricken with such tumultuous emotions in her life. Never before had another person affected her with such careless poignancy. What was it about Matthew Thatcher that made her think not only about him but about herself? She had sudden yearnings that she had never had before, and they suddenly made her question what else she yearned for that she had not been aware of. Was this what love did to a person? If it was, then she wanted nothing to do with it.

"All children read fairy tales," he paused. "Well, I didn't, but I was busy pulling the pigtails of the cutest girls in school."

He said this with a devilish grin as he pulled on a lock of her hair that had come loose from the braid she had plaited it into after her afternoon bath. The gesture was unnerving, and her chest rose and fell with the breaths she could not catch.

"I wasn't your usual child," she said. "I thought I explained that."

He looked at her quizzically now. "Explained that?"

"My father, Captain--"

"Ah, the great captain, making waves at the War Office." He grinned harder now. "Making waves." She didn't respond. "It was a bit of a jest right there, but it's all right. It's late. I understand how it could have passed you by like a ship in the--" He stopped when she still had not decided how to react. "Never mind. Your father, the captain," he finished as if to pull her thoughts back in line, which it successfully did.

"My father is a celebrated member of the War Office, and it was only expected that his progeny should do their part for the Office when the time came. Only..." she didn't know how to say this part. "Only it was never expected that Father would only produce girl children."

"He had daughters?" Thatcher said, raising an eyebrow that was clearly visible in the dim light. "You didn't explain that earlier. You said that he had just told you what was expected of you."

"Yes, daughters," Kate said. "Two of them. So it was expected that, as the eldest, I would take on--"

"So you have a little sister?" he said, and she noticed suddenly that his voice had lost its playful tone.

"Yes, Miranda. She's four years my junior, and--"

"What is she doing for the War Office?" he asked.

She let out a puff of air as if to exhibit her frustration with the numerous interruptions, but Thatcher remained oblivious. Or in the least, he just didn't mind interrupting her.

"She is not an acting agent for the War Office. She is the Duchess of Wellesley."

Now both of Thatcher's eyebrows went up. "Quite a catch for the daughter of a captain," he said. "At least, if my calculations of the ever confusing class structure in this country are accurate."

"We're in Italy. I don't know their class structure."

He frowned. "Of England, then ."

"Right," she said. "Yes, it would be rather unheard of if my father--"

"Were not who he is," Thatcher finished.

"Why do you keep doing that?"

Her frustration at being interrupted worked successfully to combat her unsettled nerves at his nearness. She wanted him to stop, but she wanted him to continue if only to survive this interview. As long as he asked nothing about her deplorable actions earlier that afternoon when she had kissed him.

Unexpectedly, he took her hand in both of his, cradling her fingers in the warmth of his touch, and her breath all but froze in her lungs.

"Because we may have precious little time in this world, and I do not wish to waste a moment of it with unnecessary dribble." And then he dropped her hand, the air rushed from her lungs, and she really did wish to sit in his lap. "I'm joshing you, Kate. There's too much to this story, and you are not going fast enough for me. So the elder daughter of the captain was expected to be an agent for the War Office?"

She nodded. "Precisely--"

"What did you expect to be?" he asked then , and her mind jerked at the change of topic.

"I beg your pardon," she said yet again.

"What. Did. You. Expect. To. Be."

He said each word with a clear space between them, and still she could not understand him.

"There was never a moment for me to expect anything other than what I was told was to happen. I have explained that already," she finally said, hoping that finished the conversation.

But Thatcher shook his head.

"That's terrible," he whispered, and it brought Kate's shoulders up, squaring off to face him.

"I beg your--" she started to say but mentally shook her head. "I would not expect someone such as yourself to understand what it means to have the honor and privilege to follow in the footsteps of one's revered father. I feel blessed to have such opportunity and occasion."

Thatcher's eyes went cold. She saw it the moment it happened even in the muted light of the horse stall. Seconds before he had been the jovial and vivid Matthew Thatcher, charmer of women on both sides of the Atlantic Ocean. But now his face was hard, his gaze unyielding, his mouth set in the distinct outline of a grimace.

"I do actually," he whispered before he stood and moved out of her stall.

He had long since settled into his own straw bed when Kate finally blinked at the spot where he had sat, wondering what he had meant by that.

CHAPTER 5

*T*he next few days passed in a welcomed blur of physical exhaustion. Kate had never known a farm could be so much work. More, she couldn't believe a house alone was so much work. She suddenly realized what the staff of her townhouse in London did during the day and resolved to give them a much needed raise. Every morning she rose in the near dark to stumble to the kitchen only to find Rosa already at work, bustling about the day's tasks. She tried very hard not to notice when Thatcher rose or where he went, welcoming the reprieve that physical exertion provided from all other thoughts.

It had been one thing when Kate feared that she was developing a dangerous attraction to Matthew Thatcher, the handsome American who had played rogue to her bar wench. It was quite another when she had grown to care for him so much that she gave his very words the power to question her own devotions. And while she struggled to figure out what it was that she'd said to elicit such a cold reaction from him, she realized she had done just that. And she couldn't let that happen. Katharine Cavanaugh was an agent for the War Office. She did not fall in love. It was not expected.

And for now, Kate concentrated on not blinking, listening to every word Rosa Salvatore said as they stood in the kitchen of the farmhouse.

"You add salt to the boiling water?" she asked then , her studied Italian nowhere near the beautiful, musical tones of that of her host.

They stood over said pot of boiling water, sweat dripping from every orifice of their bodies in ways no lady would ever admit, watching the water boil. The water had been boiling for at least three minutes, and Kate knew that they should have placed the pasta into the pot by now, but Rosa continued to talk. She let her eyes drift for a moment to the pile of fresh orecchiette that she had pressed into perfect little round ears with a thicker bit at the edges, with Rosa's guidance, of course. The pasta had taken much longer than she had expected, and Rosa had finished two batches of spaghetti while Kate made it through her single batch of orecchiette.

And if she were making pasta, then Katharine Cavanaugh was not thinking about kissing Matthew Thatcher, about sitting in his lap or about how he was not speaking to her.

As for the kiss, she had still not decided which part had been worse. The fact that she had actually given into her roiling emotions and kissed him or the fact that she had told him she had not meant it. Neither seemed like a particularly brilliant maneuver on her part, and she rather wished to forget both of them. But she could not, as it seemed all her mind was capable of then was thinking of exactly that.

Kissing Matthew Thatcher.

And then of how he was not speaking to her.

She could not honestly say what had come over her when she kissed him, but it was certainly something she had never felt before, of that she was adamant. She had simply been leaning on the table, a precise thought in her head as to what they should do, when suddenly she wanted to kiss him. Perhaps if he had not leaned forward, perhaps if he had not smiled at her, perhaps if he did not have those carved features and brilliant blue eyes, and perhaps if he were not simply there in front of her--

And as for the incident in the barn, she simply felt bad. She must have trodden on a sensitive subject for him, one she hadn't known existed but suspected related to his initial dislike of the farm. And worse, she hadn't found time to apologize for it. They barely saw one another between chores, and by the end of the day, they were often too tired to do more than bid each other good night. But she owed Thatcher an apology, and she would find the time that very day to deliver it.

For the moment, she distracted herself by cooking pasta with Rosa. And she enjoyed it.

It was odd if she truly thought on it. Kate had never spent a single day in a kitchen in her entire life. She had most definitely visited kitchens before. She did, after all, have a kitchen to run in her townhouse back in London when she was not out playing spy. So there were the times she traveled below stairs on occasion. But she had never touched anything. Had never dared. Cook would be sure to have her head if anything were moved or even altered in the slightest way in her kitchen. So Kate had visited and left, much like she would a museum. But it was not so in Rosa's kitchen. In Rosa's kitchen, Kate found herself covered in flour and smelling like a stable boy. And Rosa continued to give her further and further instruction.

And even that unsettled Kate. It was one thing to have an uncontrollable physical reaction to a man, but it was quite another to suddenly develop a flair for cooking. Before this mission, she had had one objective in her life. To be the best agent the War Office had. Now she was suddenly kissing Americans and making sheets of pasta with a little Italian woman who did not speak English, preferring to do most of her communication through hand gestures. It was all ridiculous and unnecessary. When this mission concluded, she would be Katharine Cavanaugh, War Office spy, once more, and none of this would matter. She just had to hold her resolve for a few days more.

She would seek out Matthew Thatcher today, apologize, and get on with finding a solution to their predicament. It was completely unacceptable that she had dithered this long.

Finally, Rosa pointed to the orecchiette, and Kate scooped it up, dropping it into the boiling pot of water. The pasta bounced as if suddenly coming to life, swirling about the bubbles of water. Kate carefully used a wooden spoon to separate the pasta and move it through the boiling water. With a smack on her hand from Rosa, Kate set the wooden spoon down so as not to be accused of over stirring the pot. And then Rosa was off again, moving to the other side of the kitchen, gesturing to the tomatoes they had cleaned earlier that now sat in a ceramic bowl.

Rosa expected Kate to make the garnish for their noon meal that would consist of the orecchiette and a fresh loaf of olive bread.

"But I've never made the garnish," Kate said, but Rosa only threw up her hands, muttering something about having courage.

Kate straightened as Rosa continued to give instructions, gesturing to the tomatoes and a bunch of fresh basil on the table. Seemingly finished with her instruction, Rosa placed a sharp, deadly looking knife in Kate's hand and went out the door of the kitchen. Kate finally blinked at the closed kitchen door, wondering what had just happened. She thought she had heard Rosa say she was going to call the men in from the fields for the noon meal, but the tiny woman had been moving so quickly, Kate wasn't sure what was speech and what was the sound of her body moving through air. Kate looked down at the knife she held in her hand and then at the tomatoes.

This was all just a matter of circumstance, Kate thought, as she sliced into the first tomato. She just had to remember that she was an agent for the War Office. That was her first and only objective.

* * *

MATTHEW TOOK off his borrowed hat and wiped the sweat from his brow with his forearm. Angelo Salvatore had a big head. Literally. His hat fell just a little too low on Thatcher's brow, but seeing as how the alternative was no hat at all, Thatcher made do.

The sun was full in the aqua sky, the color a reflection of the clear blue water far below in the port of Naples. He would often catch himself looking off into the distance where the blues met on the horizon and recalled a similar scene, one from a long ago time when he had been standing next to his own father and not someone else's. Thomas had been with him, his fishing rod slung over his shoulder with the day's catch. The image was so clear Thatcher almost asked the question, the question he asked over and over again from that day sixteen years ago. Why had he not listened to his father? Why had he not listened when his father had told him to watch out for Thomas?

Thatcher heard Rosa before he saw her. Her call was becoming familiar to him now, and he thought he may even be picking up a word or two of Italian. That may have been wishful thinking on his part, but it wasn't so hard for him to believe that a boy from South Carolina could learn Italian from a little old woman who dressed primarily in kerchiefs.

She called them for the noon meal, and Thatcher set the borrowed hat back on his head, looking in the direction of the house just as the little woman's head popped up over the crest. She did not hold up a hand to shield her gaze from the penetrating rays of the sun. She only stood there, hands in her apron, until she could get a clear view of Luigi and him. And then she called once more, turned about, and walked back down the hill to the farmhouse.

Thatcher hefted the basket of olives they had taken down that day while tending to one of the trees before looking to Luigi.

"I think perhaps this afternoon we look at the cow like you said," Luigi said to him, stepping off the ladder they had wedged against one of the trees. "You think she is really not happy in her stall?"

Thatcher carried the basket of olives while they walked in the direction of the house. He wasn't really sure what had been truth and what had been old farmer wisdom his father had acquired, and Thatcher had not been around long enough to ask his father the difference. So he only had the anecdotes his father had told him to guess how a farm was properly run. And that is what he had for the cow.

"I think she is giving you fits because she can't get to the fresh water and hay that you have for her without straining her neck."

His father had always told him that a cow had to be comfortable if she were to give you any of her milk. After all, why should she give you something if you gave her nothing in return? And having a relaxing environment to get her water and hay seemed like a large enough gesture to cause her to not be ornery. It was worth a try anyway. And there was enough room in the barn to adjust the animal, give her better access to the water trough and hay.

When they reached the bottom of the hill, Thatcher headed in the direction of the barn to store the olives, but Rosa stood in the area between the house and the barn, hands on her hips. Thatcher didn't understand what she said, but Luigi sighed in resignation.

"Here. Give the olives to me. My Rosa says she see a rat go into the barn. I'll go look and put these away," he finished, taking the basket from Thatcher.

Thatcher didn't dare raise his eyebrows in question, but after several nights spent using the barn as accommodations, he was quite certain there were no rats in it. But he had come to realize that Rosa Salvatore ran a very neat establishment, and if she believed there was a rat, there was going to be a very long search to find it.

Thatcher touched the brim of his hat, but Rosa only frowned at him as he made his way to the house. The darkened interior was an instant relief from the sun, and he paused a moment just inside the door, the aromas of the kitchen engulfing him like an over eager pet upon his master's return. He smelled garlic and tomato, yeast and sausage. His mouth watered, and he took off his hat, ducking past the rafter that crossed just past the door and entered the kitchen.

Kate stood at the counter along the far wall, her arms moving at her sides as if she were working on something at its surface. He stood there and stared as it was obvious she had not heard him come in. She was beautiful. Tall and solid, she stood with her back slightly bent, her braid of hair falling over one shoulder. He wanted to walk up behind her, press his lips to the back of her neck, feel her pulse beat there. He wanted to wrap his arms around her, pull her against him, feel her warmth spread through his already overheated body.

Seeing her standing there with the light from the kitchen window illuminating her like some kind of ethereal being brought back the image of her sitting in the near dark, the faded moonlight streaming over her face, highlighting the dimple on her chin that beckoned his touch. But the memory brought another one that left him unsettled, and he pushed it all aside, stepping farther into the room.

"Afternoon," he said, and Kate screamed.

He jumped at the sound, his borrowed hat dropping from his hands. He heard the clatter of something metal, and then Kate was jumping up and down. He had never actually seen a person jump and up down like that, and as Kate was nearly six feet tall, there wasn't much room in the small house for her to be doing so. And then he noticed that she had turned slightly and had one finger stuck in her mouth. He looked at the counter beyond to see a discarded knife and quickly surmised what had happened.

"Are you all right?" he said, coming over to her, gently pulling the offended finger from her mouth. It came loose with an odd sucking sound, and Thatcher brought her hand into his, examining the finger for damage. A small trickle of blood oozed from the tip just near her fingernail. He pressed it with the softest touch he could, testing the skin for breakage. There was a small slit where the skin had come away, but it looked like she had only nicked herself.

He looked up to find Kate studying her hand just as intently as he was.

"Stick this back in your mouth," he said and let go of her hand to move to the other side of the kitchen.

A small wooden chest sat on a trunk by the doorway that led to the rest of the house, and Thatcher had seen Luigi take it out a time or two to repair the small cuts he got from working the trees. Thatcher opened the lid to find bandages and various bottles of differing colors and sizes. He wondered what was in them but decided it was probably safer to just get a clean piece of bandage for Kate's finger. He tore a piece off, shut the chest, and turned back around to see Kate sucking on her finger again, watching him warily from the other side of the room.

He gestured to the table. "Sit," he said, pulling back one of the chairs.

He saw the way her eyes drifted from his face to the chair and back and raised his eyebrows at her hesitation. She moved then without speaking, whether because she didn't trust him with her wounded finger or because said finger was jammed into her mouth, he couldn't decide. He went over to the stove, checking the pot of boiling water Rosa always kept on the flame in case it was needed. He dipped some into a cup and returned to the table, taking a seat opposite Kate.

"Here," he said, gesturing to the hand stuck in her mouth.

She cautiously withdrew the finger, once again causing that odd sucking sound to vibrate through the air. He took her hand in his and, for the first time, noticed the contrast in their skin tones. Her skin was luminous, the white hue so pale it radiated with light against the tanned skin of his hand. But while he held her hand, he also noticed how cracked and torn her fingernails were. Thatcher had once heard his mother say that you could tell a gentleman by his shoes and a lady by her hands. If anyone were to judge the Countess of Stirling just then , they would surely not find her to be a true lady. He wondered then what she had been doing for the past week. He had never thought before then that she must be doing something to keep herself busy during the days. She was tired enough when they both retired to their quarters in the barn, so it wasn't as if she were lazing about all day. He felt ashamed for not thinking to ask her what it was she had been tasked with while he was helping Luigi with the farm.

He tested the cup of water, finding it had cooled enough to the touch that it may be safe for him to wash her cut with. Taking a bowl from the stack that Rosa left on the table, he placed it under her finger before picking up the cup and gently dribbling the warm water over the cut, hoping the running water would flush anything that had gotten into the cut that may cause it to become inflamed later. He felt her flinch and looked up, expecting to find her holding back a scream, but instead he found her watching him intently, her face perfectly relaxed.

She blinked up at him as if she could feel him watching her. "I wasn't expecting the water to be so warm," she said as if she knew he had questioned her reaction.

He nodded and finished with the water, shaking her hand slightly over the bowl to dislodge any water droplets before applying the bandage. She didn't say anything further as he wrapped the bandage around her finger, tucking the end in, so it wouldn't come loose. He patted her hand when he was finished but for whatever reason, found it hard to let go of it. He looked up to find Kate watching him, her hazel eyes endless pools in the weak light of the kitchen.

Once more they were each leaning precariously across the surface of the table, she to extend her arm far enough for him to apply the bandage, and he so he could reach her to apply it. And he thought for a moment that he could lean forward and kiss her like she had done only days before. But then they had just been two professionals on an assignment together. Now there was something between them, and he laid her hand back down on the table, his fingers sliding along the length of hers until finally there was no more to hold onto. He felt the disconnect like a punch to his stomach, and he drew in a large breath to cover the sensation.

It was for the best. It had to be. She didn't want marriage, and he didn't want connection of any kind. It would be wise not to instigate the compulsion to be with her.

He smiled at her, though, hoping if he were just himself with her again, he wouldn't need to apologize for his behavior earlier that week. That they could go on the way they were before, accidental companions in a war-torn country that spoke a language he did not understand. But Kate continued to stare at him, her hand still in the place where he had set it on the table, the now bandaged finger looking oddly out of place. Her mouth parted just the slightest bit, and for a moment, he thought she would say something. But when she didn't, her expression slipped into one that reminded Thatcher of the look his brother some-times gave him when he would leave the farmhouse in the morning to do chores. It was a look of forlorn confusion, but the person giving the look was too proud to show the way he really felt, which was somewhere between misunder-standing and abandonment. And just then , Thatcher knew he needed to apologize.

"About the other night,-"

"I'm sorry I upset you--"

They both spoke at the same time, stopping when they heard each other's words.

"I'd better go first," Thatcher said, not wanting to hear an apology from Kate for his poor actions. "I'm sorry I behaved badly the other night. There was no way for you to know that the topic of conversation troubled me. I hope you can accept my apology."

Kate licked her lips, a gesture he was starting to relate to her gathering her courage.

"I'm sorry as well," she said. "I should have asked you what was bothering you."

He tilted his head at her words. "What was bothering me?"

She nodded. "There's something about this farm that you don't like, and I have a feeling it has to do with your family or something. It's not my place to pry, but I do want you to know that I'm here if you need someone to talk to. But again, I do not wish to pry as your private thoughts are yours, and I have no right to them."

"Someone to talk to?" Thatcher said, and he thought Kate might have blushed if it had not been so hot in the kitchen so as to provide an excuse for her suddenly flushed face.

"As unfortunate as it is, you and I only have each other in this thing. That is unless we ask Luigi for help," she said, and he nodded before she quite finished.

Her words tickled at a fear he kept safely tucked away. He was responsible for no one and no one for him. He should probably correct her on that point, but he said something else instead, completely avoiding everything his mind told him.

"About asking Luigi for help." He leaned back in his chair, the space between them growing uncomfortably large. "I think it's a wise idea."

Kate nodded.

"I agree. I think Luigi has a solid network of allegiances amongst the farmers," she said then.

Thatcher raised an eyebrow.

"Every day a child will come into the yard. Rosa will take some of the food she's made and exchange it with the child for whatever it is that the child has brought. Sometimes it's cloth, sometimes it's buttons, and once it was even a wheel of cheese."

Thatcher sat up straighter. "The farmers are looking out for one another."

Kate nodded. "And if the farmers are so connected--"

"It's a veritable web of information," Thatcher finished the sentence.

And Kate nodded, a satisfied smile on her lips. "Someone must know what's happening. Someone must hear where Murat and his men are planning to be and when."

Kate's face lit the further she delved into her story, and for the first time, Thatcher realized it was more than expectation that drove Kate in her career as a War Office agent. She was actually good at it. This knowledge sent a thrill through him he had not expected, and the muscles in his abdomen clenched at the thought.

"Asking Luigi for aid in obtaining information from fellow farmers would prove to be wise given the evidence at hand. And more, in the circumstances, it is our only option, and no matter what should occur, it will then be our best option. We should be able to handle any consequences. Is that not true, Thatcher?"

Thatcher watched her eyes, their warm hazel hues toying with his attention.

"I reckon," he said.

And then he stood up, pushing back from the table. He watched Kate as she watched him round the end of the table and come over to her. Without hesitation he pulled her up from her chair, his arms locking tightly around her once she was standing.

"As long as we're both aware of all of the consequences," he said just before he kissed her.

CHAPTER 6

ate tensed, whether from the shock of his abrupt touch or the feel of his lips on hers, she couldn't be sure. But when the shock faded, she felt an entirely new set of tumultuous emotions. Warmth. Hunger. Want. Desire. Those were the ones she could name at least. But the burning, low in her stomach, that seeped down into her legs and ran up and into her arms, it was all too much, too much of something she couldn't name.

But she liked it. Of that, she was certain.

Her arms were trapped between them, and she wiggled enough to free them, sliding them around Thatcher's waist, her fingers digging into his back as if to hold on for her very life. She was slipping, falling, while she stood, securely locked in his embrace. The sensation was unnerving, and she hoped it never ended. And as the shock that she was honestly and truly kissing this man disappeared, her conscious mind came roaring back, a surge of energy spreading through her body as she realized what was happening.

It was not that she had never been kissed before like this.

It was not that she had never been held in a man's arms. It was just that it had never been real. She could recall far more scandalous embraces she had shared with the Earl of Stryden, her sometimes partner on various War Office assignments, but they had meant nothing. Still meant nothing, and she was certain one day she would forget them entirely, for they had all been a charade.

This was real. Thatcher was real. And more, he honestly wanted to kiss her. He honestly wanted to be there in that moment, his lips locked on hers.

He wanted her.

The realization was startling, and she felt that surge of shock again, a numbness sweeping through her limbs as her fingers dug deeper into the muscles of his back.

She became aware of other things then . The smell of wood and sweat and sheer man that exuded from him. The way his beard scraped along the skin of her cheeks and chin. The slight roughness to his lips, dry from a morning spent in the sun. She became aware of his hands that had gripped her shoulders but now slid down her back, moving slowly, achingly slowly, downward along her spine, his fingers following the precise ridge of bone until she thought she couldn't stand the touch any longer. But then he stopped, his hands coming to rest on the curve of her buttocks.

And for just a moment, she wanted his hands to dip lower. Push further into impropriety. The thought itself was enough to have her squirming, but whether she was squirming toward him or away from him, she wasn't sure.

But for a stunning moment, she realized she wanted this, too.

Katharine Cavanaugh wanted this, and it had nothing to do with any of the rules her mother had laid out or the expectations her father had set before her. This was all about Kate, and it was about Kate being there in that moment with

Thatcher. And she wanted this, whatever it was that was happening between them.

But then the thought stopped there.

What was she supposed to do with him?

She stood there, her hands pressed into his back, his hands on the crest of her buttocks, their lips locked in a torrent of heat, and she didn't know how to proceed.

From a purely physical standpoint, she knew her body would tell her what felt good and what didn't, and she had certainly stumbled across enough encounters in her spying to know what could happen next between a man and a woman. But this was an emotional thing. A husband had never played into the expectations that had been drilled into her since her youth. There had never been room for such a thought.

But what if there was?

The fact that the question had even formed in her mind shook her to her very core. And Kate suddenly didn't know how to feel about that. For the first time in her life, she questioned the very existence she had come to understand was absolute. But standing in Rosa Salvatore's kitchen in the arms of a man who sent her emotions spiraling, nothing about that existence seemed absolute in the least.

What if this kiss led to more? What if Thatcher wanted more? What if she did? What was she to do?

Did spies take lovers? Lovers were less demanding than husbands, she supposed.

But then Thatcher moved, deepening the kiss, and Kate was lost. Rational thought scattered like a flock of disturbed birds. Thatcher's hands had moved lower, cupping her buttocks now and fitting her tightly against him. She felt the full length of him, from his muscled chest to his hard thighs, pressing against her. And she clung, the physical sensations overpowering any chance she had at thinking about this rationally.

It was all so hot, literally. The heat of his body, the heat of his mouth on hers, it all enveloped her until she was afraid she couldn't take it any longer. But just as she thought she was at the breaking point, something shifted. Maybe it was him or maybe it was her, but suddenly she could breathe. Only now, she didn't feel as connected to the ground. Had he lifted her up? Surely not. She was nearly six feet tall. A man did not just lift a woman of her stature off her feet. Did he?

But then she felt the unmistakable press of a table against the backs of her thighs and then she was sitting on the kitchen table as he stepped between her legs. The idea that she should be sitting in such a vulnerable position in the middle of a compromised assignment should have alerted her to all of the negative things that were happening in that situation, but then Thatcher's tongue slipped into her mouth, and she forgot everything and clung.

Her hands came around from his back, slipped up the contour of his chest to wrap around his neck, pulling his head down closer as if he could get any closer. She didn't know how she knew to do this, but she guessed it was sheer instinct driving her forward. And Thatcher responded with a sound she had never heard a gentleman make. It was a base, guttural sound deep within his throat. She felt it vibrate against her forearms, and the knowledge that she had made him sound so animalistic had her wrapping her legs around his waist in triumph.

He tilted the angle of his head, his mouth nipping at the corner of her lips. The pressure was teasing, and she strained to regain the unbearable contact of moments before. But he was unrelenting in his teasing, moving along her jaw and down her throat. The pain that had begun as a simmering burn low in her stomach traveled deeper, sparking into a fire that she feared would consume her. And worse, she didn't know what it meant. She had never felt like this before. Was something wrong? Was she supposed to feel this way?

And when Thatcher's teeth settled on the delicate line of her collarbone, she cracked, her hands coming to rest on his chest, pushing as hard as she could until he fell backward, stumbling on his feet. He was breathing hard, his eyes a glassy abyss she was sure mirrored her own.

"What's happening?" she said, the only words she could summon. "What are you doing to me?"

And at first, Thatcher didn't say anything. She watched him draw ragged breaths until his eyes cleared, his gaze sharpening to a point, a point directed entirely at her. And then something changed. It was subtle, but she marked it like she would if he'd suddenly decided to shave his head of all its glorious blond curls. It was a hardening, a veil of stoicism falling over his face. His hands dropped to his sides, still in their place. And then he said something that Kate felt more deeply than any of his kisses.

"I'm sorry," he said and then worse, he dragged an arm over his mouth as if to wipe it clean of the impression of her kiss.

Her breath froze in her chest. Her body, so hot just seconds before, went as cold as the rain in London.

"What?" she said, her mind not understanding what was happening.

He was sorry? That was his response? Sorry for what? Sorry for forcing himself on her? Sorry that it had happened at all?

She didn't know what to do. She didn't know what to say. She didn't know what to feel. And her brain wasn't functioning. She knew that there must have been a misunder-standing. She knew that he must have done or said something wrong.

But what if it was she who had it wrong?

She had only known Matthew Thatcher for a few weeks. For all appearances, he could have been the most popular rake in London. She wouldn't and couldn't have any reason to know that. Perhaps, he was just looking for his next conquest, and she had been available.

But even as she thought it, she pushed it aside. Matthew Thatcher wasn't like that. He wouldn't do that to her.

"I'm sorry. I can't--" Thatcher said, but his words faltered.

His voice carried just the slightest bit of hesitation as he still struggled to even out his breathing, but otherwise, it was the same old drawl that she had come to expect from Matthew Thatcher. It was as if nothing had happened at all.

She must be the one who had it wrong, but then he made it just the slightest bit...worse.

"I'm truly sorry, Kate, but I can't let this happen," he said.

She wanted to ask him what it was that was happening, because she would certainly like to know, but just then she became aware of something else. A noise that was somehow familiar and yet it couldn't be as they had only been at the Salvatores' for a week. Nothing should be familiar to her there. But then she knew.

"There's someone in the yard," she said.

And just like that, her mind was wiped clean. Her training kicked in, and she hopped off the table, her instincts as an agent telling her to get ready for whatever was coming next. Thatcher moved as well, going to the only window in the room and carefully peering at an angle through it so as not to be seen.

"It looks like we have company," he said.

Kate straightened her dress. "How many and what size?"

Thatcher turned to look at her, one eyebrow raised. "I fail

to see how size is relevant, but it's a gentleman and a young girl."

"Blonde pig tails?" she asked, remembering one particular child that often appeared in the yard.

Thatcher nodded. "Looks like. Gentleman farmer it would appear. Taller than Luigi and definitely rounder in the chest."

"How do you know he's taller than Luigi?"

Thatcher turned toward her. "Because Luigi is standing next to him, and they're coming this way."

He started to move even before he had finished his sentence.

"You've been in this house more than me. Where can we hide?"

He took her elbow in his grip as if to steer her, and for the slimmest of moments, she remembered the burn of his touch before she drove it from her mind.

"This way," she said and pulled him down the only corridor leading off of the kitchen.

She did not have far to go before stopping at a cupboard a few paces down the hallway. Rosa stored her linens in the tiny cupboard and shelves took up most of the space. But she knew there would perhaps be room for two just inside the door.

Perhaps.

She pulled open the door and felt Thatcher's hesitation.

"Well, I reckon we've been closer before this," he said and yanked her inside the cupboard with him, pulling the door shut behind them.

* * *

THATCHER HEARD when Luigi entered with the stranger and what was presumably the stranger's daughter because the two men were having an unusually loud discussion about garlic bulbs. He knew it was about garlic bulbs, because the two men conversed in English. The sound of the stilted words from men he knew could probably speak more easily in Italian alerted Thatcher to the possibility that this may not have been a normal house call.

"But it does not have the zest if you roast over long in the oil. You must take it out sooner," said a gravelly, unfamiliar voice that Thatcher assumed belonged to the stranger.

Luigi went to say something, but the sound of the door opening cut off his words. Thatcher adjusted so his ear pressed more evenly to the cupboard door, but it also meant he was then pressed more firmly to the very enticing backside of the Countess of Stirling. Feeling every curve of her body against his reminded him of just what an idiot he had been. When he had pulled her out of her chair and kissed her, he had not really been thinking much beyond the physical act of the thing. He had suddenly needed to kiss her, and he had thought she needed the same. But then she had pushed him away, and he realized how incredibly stupid he was.

She didn't want the burden of a relationship any more than he did. He had been stupid to forget that.

Kate wiggled against him, her own ear pressed to the wood of the door. He would have scowled at her if she had been able to see him. As it was, he scowled at the top of her head.

He returned his attention to the room beyond and heard the distinct sound of the door now closing. And there was Rosa's voice, speaking in Italian, and when neither of the two men responded, Thatcher assumed she was speaking to the little girl. And then there was the scrape of chairs being pulled back, and Thatcher imagined the two men sitting down at the table.

"What is it, Alberto?"

This was from Luigi, again in English. Thatcher wondered if they spoke in a language foreign to them so Rosa and the little girl would not understand what was being said. He strained closer to the door, his instincts perking up.

"It is Murat. He is coming," said the other man.

Kate poked him, a single hard thrust of her elbow into his abdomen as if to say she was right about Murat doing something stupid, reminding him once more of just what a good spy she was.

"They say he is coming to ensure control of Naples. There is to be a battle here in the hillside."

"But this does not make sense. Murat has an understanding with Austria to maintain the throne of Naples."

There was a sound like plates striking the table, and the voices ceased, except for scattered words in Italian that Thatcher believed related to the meal that was likely being laid before them.

"And how likely is the word of Austria to hold now that Napoleon has escaped Elba?"

There was silence after this statement, only the sounds of a meal being consumed filled the space. Thatcher heard the muffled sounds of Kate's breathing and suddenly wondered how loud his own had become. He was concentrating so hard on the voices beyond that he had scarcely noticed what was happening in the cupboard. Not that he could entirely forget who it was that was pressed so intimately against him.

"Murat would turn on his brother-in-law then ? What of Caroline?" Luigi suddenly asked in English.

Thatcher would need to confirm with Kate, but he thought Caroline to be Napoleon's sister, Murat's wife.

"How much do you care for your in-laws? But that is not it at all. Murat has realigned his allegiance with Napoleon."

More clattering of dishes.

"Then Murat expects war with the Austrians?"

This was from Luigi, or at least Thatcher thought it was. The man's voice had become noticeably quieter, and Thatcher strained to hear him.

"Yes, it will be a battle with the Austrians. Murat must hold the throne."

This was followed by a burst of feminine laughter, the sound clashing with the serious tone of the men, but the sounds quieted all too quickly.

"We are to prepare for a battle then ," came from Luigi.

"I'm afraid so, friend," said the stranger.

"But when?" Luigi asked, but the response was cut off as the talk quickly lapsed into Italian, and Thatcher thought the conversation had changed. There was the scraping of chairs, and Thatcher thought the young girl and Rosa had joined the men at the table. There was no further talk of the impending battle unless it was in the Italian he did not understand.

But then Kate started to wiggle against him, her body turning so that her lips pressed against his ear.

"I told you Murat would do something rash," she whispered.

He was distracted momentarily by the thrill the feel of her warm breath on his skin gave him, but her words snapped him out of it with unnecessary haste. He tilted his own head to bring his lips against her ear, whispering, "I must commend you for your excellent spying abilities. You have a real knack for it. What do you think we should do next?"

He expected some sort of strong reply, but when he was met with only silence, he tilted his head more to look at her face. The cupboard was too dark, however, and he could only make out the dim outline of the shape of her face. But when she continued to say nothing, he poked her.

"Ow," she hissed, the sound more like escaping air than an

actual word. "I think we should get out of this cupboard," she said.

Thatcher could not agree more, but it was not as if they could simply leave. From the sounds coming from beyond the door, the stranger and the little girl were still heavily involved with the meal Rosa had been preparing. Or perhaps it was Kate who had been preparing it. He looked down at the fuzzy shape of her head again, wondering again just what it was she did during the day when he was out doing chores as Luigi called it.

"What about the guests?" he whispered back, moving his head ever so slightly in the direction of the kitchen as if she could understand his meaning.

He thought she might have frowned at him, but as he couldn't really see her, he wasn't sure.

"We'll have to wait for them to leave, I suppose," she said. "When do you think Murat and his men will move in?"

Thatcher shook his head.

"I'm not sure. It's not as if Napoleon has been out that long. How long does it take for a country to move around their armies?"

He felt more than saw Kate shake her head.

"You make it all sound like some sort of childish game," she said, although her tone held no malice, only a tinge of regret.

"I wonder who that man is," Thatcher said then , pressing his ear to the cupboard door once more.

"I believe he's a neighboring farmer. I've seen that girl more than once here at the house."

Thatcher pulled his head away from the door so quickly he collided with the shelves behind him.

"You have? Why?"

Kate might have shrugged but the lack of space prevented the gesture from fully materializing.

"She's one of the children who brings something in exchange for Rosa's cooking."

Thatcher nodded, recalling her statement from earlier about the farmers being in allegiance with one another.

"Is that where all of those socks came from?" he asked, remembering a bundle of socks that had suddenly appeared on the kitchen table one day.

"Mmm," was all Kate said, her ear returning once more to the door.

There was nothing but the usual sounds of a group of people partaking of a meal. There was some chatter, but it was often followed by the sound of a young girl's laugh, so Thatcher assumed it was nothing of a serious nature.

"Have you thought about what we'll do when we get to the Alps? Do you expect me to climb mountains to get back to England?" Kate suddenly asked.

Thatcher raised an eyebrow that was completely lost on its intended.

"I would enjoy seeing you climb mountains just for the sheer pleasure of the sight, but I don't think it will be necessary. If there's a battle on land, we can escape by sea. Didn't Luigi say his sons and their families had gone to Sicily?"

Kate nodded again. "Sicily is being heavily guarded by the British navy. Do you think we could make it?"

She turned her head, and her hair brushed against his chin. He caught the scent of soap as she turned into him. He knew she had asked him something, but he had completely forgotten what it was. He could just make out the shape of her eyes, blinking up at him, her mouth slightly parted in wonder. And for just a moment, he wondered if she had forgotten what she had asked as well.

"Perhaps. If the confusion were great enough," his voice was so low he hoped she heard it.

She was beautiful, standing there in a cupboard with him,

her body pressed against his. And the feeling of regret that he had so adamantly pushed away rose again, scraping at his resolve. He wanted to kiss her again. He wanted to kiss her like he had before, her body wrapped around his so tightly he didn't know where she ended and he began. But he knew even as he felt it, that it would be wrong. He couldn't let it happen. He couldn't let her get that close. Hell, she hadn't even imagined having a man as a part of her life. But, God, why did she have to look at him like that? And why did he have to care so much?

He bent his head, torturing himself by bringing his lips so close to hers. And then she moved, too, or maybe he just imagined it, but her lips were closer to his now, and he could almost taste her.

And then someone opened the door, and he fell with an utter lack of grace to the floor beyond.

* * *

"Is it a common practice to hide in cupboards in England?" Luigi asked.

Kate looked up through the mess of her braid at the short Italian man leaning over them. She had thankfully only landed partially on Thatcher, the majority of her body making contact with the hard wooden floor. She was used to such things happening to her and doubted she would even feel the remnants of the fall later, but she did feel the embarrassment such a position entailed. She pushed her braid out of her face and went to stand, only to feel a warm hand take hold of her arm and lift her neatly to her feet with what appeared to be very little effort.

When she had righted herself, she looked about to see who it was that had helped her only to find herself staring into the warm brown eyes of the man Luigi had called

Alberto. If she had had any misgivings about enlisting the help of Luigi's friends in their attempts to escape with whatever information they could, it was now a moot point for it was obvious that more than just the Salvatores knew of their existence.

She quickly looked past the man who had helped her up only to notice the kitchen had emptied. Rosa must have gone outside with the little girl at one point. She bit her bottom lip, disappointed that she had let herself get so distracted by Thatcher in the cupboard. Everything was going along fine until he had almost tried to kiss her at the end there. But had he tried to kiss her? She didn't really know. He had clearly not enjoyed it the first time or he wouldn't have apologized for it.

And then there was the stranger that stood before her, a new vulnerability in their armor. She paused, her mouth most definitely hanging open, as she stared at the man, a slew of ramifications running through her mind at what this would mean. No one had come searching for them since their escape from the prison in the port. She had thought it odd at first, but when Luigi had explained that the man in charge was a general of Murat's army, it had not seemed so odd. A pair of ill-dressed interlopers was not something of concern when it came to the larger necessity of keeping Austria away from Murat's precious crown.

And then Thatcher got to his feet beside her, and without hesitation, he stuck out his hand in greeting to Alberto.

"Matthew Thatcher," he said, "Pleasure to make your acquaintance."

His drawl was thick, his smile charming, and not for the first time, Kate wondered if he had control over just how carefully he applied either of those impossible characteristics.

"And you must be Alberto, was it?" Thatcher added, looking to Luigi.

Luigi nodded. "Yes, this is Alberto Rossi. He lives two farms over along the main hilltop pass."

Luigi gestured as if they could see through the walls of the house to the exact part of the pass of which he spoke. Kate followed the direction of his gesture anyway, her momentary shock not wearing off as she had hoped.

"I hear there's to be a battle then ," Thatcher continued, and Kate looked at him, wondering when he had taken over control of this mission.

She thought she should feel slighted or at best, frustrated, but there was something oddly pleasing in the way Thatcher took to espionage. She had never met a gentleman who so easily slipped into the role as he did, and this fact left her questioning his place in her life. Why she questioned it, she couldn't say, but like so many times in the past few days, she felt vaguely uncertain about some of the choices she had made in her life.

"Yes, friend, it appears so. Murat is determined to hold his crown," Alberto said.

"Do you have any idea when this battle is to happen?" Thatcher asked.

Luigi interjected now, "I think perhaps we should explain to Alberto who exactly you are. I have only told him as much that you are unexpected visitors here."

Thatcher nodded. Kate opened her mouth to introduce herself, but instead of words coming out of her mouth, her stomach suddenly grumbled in protest, having been denied the meal she had so carefully prepared. She looked down at her stomach as if she could see exactly from where the offending noise had originated, but all she saw were the voluminous folds of her too big gown. She looked up quickly to find Thatcher looking at her stomach as well, and she wanted to move her hands to cover it but knew it would only make it worse.

"I reckon we should probably sit down to a meal and get to know one another. What do you think, Lady Stirling?"

She looked at Thatcher, felt the penetration of his captivating smile.

"I think that's a wonderful idea, Mr. Thatcher," she said.

CHAPTER 7

hatcher couldn't decide if Alberto Rossi was a large man or if he was just large in comparison to Luigi. As Thatcher sat across from him at the Salvatores' table, he couldn't help but notice the size of the man's knuckles. They were round and hard like small rocks with flecks of golden hair across them. They were the hands of a farmer, and Thatcher felt a twinge of memory pull at him as he saw his own father's hands. He and Thomas had watched their father so many times, each of them wondering what it was going to be like when they would run the farm. But now Thomas was dead, and Thatcher was never going back to South Carolina.

"Murat plans to take on the Austrian forces in Naples by the first of May," Thatcher said, summarizing their conversation with Mr. Rossi so far.

Out of the corner of his eye, he saw Kate spoon a large mound of little round pastas into her mouth. They were smothered in fresh tomato and onions and basil and what looked like sautéed garlic. She shoveled in another mouthful even before the first had been completely chewed and swallowed. Instead of being repulsed at the sight, his mouth watered. He was too busy speaking to Mr. Rossi to take a bite of his own food.

Mr. Rossi nodded in response to Thatcher's summary.

"That is what is being said in the port," the other man said.

Thatcher moved his gaze away from Kate, focusing on the man across from him. Like Luigi, his English was good but practiced, the language of a speaker foreign to the shapes and sounds of its vowels and consonants.

"Who is saying it in the port?" Thatcher asked, and Kate finally looked up from her bowl.

He thought she was rejoining the conversation when she grabbed for a hunk of bread from the platter set in the middle of the table. She used it to soak up the juices on her plate, the bread so succulent by the time she was done dredging it across her plate, it made an ungainly sucking sound as she pulled it away from the plate and toward her mouth. Thatcher licked his lips. He couldn't help it.

"The traders," Alberto said. "Murat plans to land a force by sea, and the traders do not want their cargos in peril. They will move their ships before the battle commences."

Kate finally interrupted, apparently taking a long enough break in her thorough consumption of her noon meal to see to the matter of espionage at hand. "A force by sea? Murat has a navy?"

Thatcher looked at her, raising an eyebrow. "The last intelligence out of Paris was that Murat was largely on his own down here. He may have sworn allegiance to his brother-in-law, but Naples is a very long way from Paris."

Thatcher looked at Alberto.

"There is belief that the navy is in fact Napoleon's."

Kate shook her head. "If it is Napoleon's, it must not be very large. Or adequate even."

Thatcher only looked at her.

"I'm assuming based on past experience. The British navy has thoroughly trounced Napoleon's fleet on more than one occasion. I'm just saying it's highly unlikely that any force Murat brings to the shores of Naples will meet with success."

She shrugged then and resumed her eating. Thatcher looked back at Alberto to find a huge grin spread across the man's face.

"You think Murat will not be successful? You think Austria will free Naples of his rule?"

Thatcher put up both hands as if in surrender.

"Now, we didn't say that," he paused long enough to glare at Kate, who studiously ate her pasta. "We're just saying it's our educated opinion that a naval attack is unlikely to have impact."

"I beg your pardon." Kate suddenly looked up from her bowl. "It is my educated opinion that a naval attack by the French will not be successful at Naples."

Thatcher watched her face for a moment, and he thought he saw just the barest hint of resolve there, a resolve he had come to expect from his companion. Katharine Cavanaugh may not have ever thought about the typical things most women thought of, but she had damn sure covered the topics of espionage more than once as she proved time and again. He looked her over carefully once more before returning to the conversation at the table.

"It is Lady Stirling's educated opinion that a naval attack will not meet with success," Thatcher clarified.

Luigi, who had been sitting quietly at the end of the table for some time, finally sat up.

"Which of the traders is it that knows of Murat's attack?"

Alberto turned slightly in his chair. "It is Scevola's league," Alberto said.

Luigi looked quickly at Thatcher. "Where did he hear it from?"

Alberto shrugged. "My only guess would be that he heard it from the British," Alberto answered.

Kate dropped her fork. Thatcher wasn't looking at her to know for certain, but he assumed that was the only thing that could make the clatter he heard just beyond his shoulder. He didn't bother to look at her. He knew she had eaten enough to move her attention elsewhere for a time.

"British?" Thatcher asked.

Alberto and Luigi both nodded.

"Scevola is the only trader in the port with permission to trade at Sicily," Luigi said, "Sometimes he brings back more than just gold in exchange for his wares. Sometimes he brings back information."

Thatcher felt Kate move behind him and wondered if the tension was getting to her. He already felt like shouting at the two men to stop being so cryptic and get on with the story. What was it that Scevola knew and how was it that he had access to such information?

"Who is Scevola?" Thatcher asked when it became apparent that the two men were not going to elaborate.

Luigi looked at Alberto, but the other man gestured to Luigi to continue.

"Scevola Amoretto is a wealthy trader here in Naples. His family is very old and well respected, but his riches, they are new. In his youth, he secured several, what is the word?" Luigi turned to Alberto who only shrugged, but it seemed to be enough as Luigi continued, "Contracts. Trading contracts from the mainland to the islands. It made him a very rich man very quickly, but there was always a shadow over his house. His methods were not of good Christian morals," Luigi said, and with an exhalation, the old man cast a wary glance at Kate.

Thatcher looked over to Kate to find her leaning on the

table, her face intent on the conversation. Only now she blinked as everyone turned to look at her.

"Is there something the matter?" she said, licking her lips as she had habit to do.

Luigi coughed uncomfortably as Alberto twitched in his seat.

"The subject is delicate enough for masculine ears. I do not wish to say in front of a lady."

Thatcher turned back to Luigi and Alberto. "I think it's safe to say it in front of Kate. There isn't much she hasn't heard."

Kate punched him lightly in the shoulder. "That is a bold assumption to make, Mr. Thatcher. We have only been of acquaintance for little more than three weeks. How can you know so much about my person?"

Thatcher looked her over briefly and simply raised an eyebrow, which earned him a muffled harrumph, but she crossed her arms over her chest and sat back in her chair, her expression dubious.

"Go ahead, Luigi, I assure you it's fine."

But even with Thatcher's insistence that Kate's reputation would not be tarnished with whatever it was the man had to say, Luigi still hesitated. He looked once at Alberto, but Alberto only pushed up his hands as if to say the matter was no longer his to control. So Luigi swallowed and looked directly at Thatcher as if by avoiding Kate's gaze, he could not be blamed for sullying her good name.

"It is rumored that Scevola Amoretto has unchristian relationships with gentlemen in powerful positions to secure generous trades," Luigi finally said.

Thatcher blinked at the man, his words not coming together in his head. With such a lead up, Thatcher had expected the revelation of the greatest sin known to man. What he was not expecting was what Luigi had actually said.

"I beg your pardon?" he finally asked.

"You're saying Scevola has intimate relationships with men in advantageous positions to get the good trading contracts in the Mediterranean," Kate said from beside him, her tone flat and unquestioning.

Luigi and Alberto both avoided looking at her, their only indication that they had even heard her was the almost imperceptible nod they cast nearly simultaneously in her direction. Kate scoffed.

"Oh, for God's sake, is that all?" she said, leaning forward once more on the table. "With all of your back and forth, I expected him to be selling state secrets to Satan himself. What bother is it of mine how Scevola spends his leisure time? I have an obligation to return to England as an agent of the War Office, and if my return also includes the effective gathering of intelligence on the movement of Murat's forces in enemy territory, then all the better. This does not leave me with even a moment to be concerned over Scevola Amoretto's nightly charades. Now then , gentlemen, how is it we can make the acquaintance of Mr. Amoretto?"

Thatcher smirked at Luigi and Alberto who sat blinking at Katharine Cavanaugh.

Finally Luigi spoke, "There is the feast of San Gennaro."

Thatcher turned to look at him. "San Gennaro?"

Luigi and Alberto nodded as Alberto picked up the story. "Always in the spring, Scevola holds a festival in the port to celebrate the patron saint of our home, San Gennaro."

Here Alberto interrupted, "And true to his unchristian ways, holding the festival on the twenty first day of April like a heathen and not on the nineteenth of September as the Church would have it."

Luigi nodded profusely through this entire statement before continuing, "There is a festival in the port. Charades and games and food, far more than the people of Naples can ever absorb. But Scevola, he does it every spring, and every spring he expects the people of Naples to adore him and his faith to San Gennaro, and all the time, we hang our heads in shame for him. But as good Christians, we do not ignore the feast in honor of a saint."

Both men crossed themselves, the movement so natural Thatcher wondered if either of them realized they had done it.

"We go to the festival, we eat the food, we celebrate San Gennaro."

Alberto nodded solemnly in agreement.

"But a festival in the port? Surely Scevola is not there? I sense he would not lower himself to mingle with common-ers," Kate said, and Thatcher looked over at the harshness of her words.

She leaned against the table, her head held in her hand as she stared intently at the two men, and Thatcher realized she was so far into the story, she was speaking in the language of its players. He looked back to Luigi and Alberto to find them also leaning on the table, apparently Kate's theatrical pull bringing them closer to the heart of the story as well. Thatcher watched in amusement.

"Oh no, Scevola may have come from us, but he wishes not to be with us. He stays at the house on the hillside for the masquerade."

Kate sat up straight with a jolt, sending Thatcher back in his chair as he had not expected her to move quite so suddenly.

"Masquerade?" she asked, her voice vibrant with what could only be called innovation.

Kate had thought of something with the pronouncement of that single word. Thatcher knew it.

"Yes, Scevola invites only the most select members of Naples' families to attend the masquerade at his home. It is a gala so extravagant, the folk in the port at the commoners' festival can see it quite clearly as if his only intention is to mock the rest of us."

Alberto crossed his arms over his chest, his forehead drooping into a menacing frown.

"That is absurd. Has the man no manners?" Kate asked.

Luigi shook his head.

"So Scevola will be holding court at this masquerade on the twenty first of April," Kate said and suddenly placed a hand on Thatcher's arm.

He had rolled up his sleeves earlier that morning as he had set to work next to Luigi, and her fingers made contact with his bare skin. Her touch was liquid heat against his skin, pouring over him in a flash he couldn't have stopped. He barely subdued the near jerk of his arm as her fingers closed about him. As it was, his muscles twitched at her touch, and his heart picked up a beat he had not meant it to.

"But that only gives us six days to prepare," Kate said, her voice a breathy whisper he thought was directed at him, but her gaze drifted over his shoulder as if she were preparing plans in her head.

Thatcher swallowed. For anyone as dramatic as Katharine Cavanaugh to be making plans, plans that likely involved him, the situation could not be good. He could imagine many a scenario that involved everything from bar wenches to impersonating a priest. He was sure the latter would be attempted before their mission was over.

"Prepare?" Thatcher dared to ask, and Kate beamed at him before leaning once more across the table in the general direction of the other two men.

"Luigi, we will need costumes for the masquerade. If we are to get close enough to Scevola to intercept any information of value, we must be unrecognizable. If we are seen and deemed intruders, we could get sent back to the prison cell in the port, and that would not help any of us. Can you help us?"

Luigi had started nodding at costumes, so Thatcher sat back, waiting to see what would happen.

"Alberto's wife, she is a terrific seamstress. She will make you and Mr. Thatcher costumes. No one will know who you are. They will be beautiful."

Thatcher immediately pictured himself in a beautiful costume and felt the need to check the remainder of his manhood, should there be any after he was rescued from Dover by a bar wench.

"Excellent!" Kate said, turning to Alberto. "It appears, Mr. Rossi, that we have need of your family's services. The British War Office would be ever in your debt."

Thatcher thought Alberto blushed at the words, but perhaps it was just the awkward light in the room. Finally, Kate turned to him, and Thatcher awarded her with a dual eyebrow raising.

"Mr. Thatcher, would you be so kind as to act as my escort to the San Gennaro masquerade on the twenty first?"

"I reckon it will be the most exciting night of my life," he said.

* * *

THE MOON HAD long since risen by the time Kate let herself out of the back door of the Salvatores' farmhouse. Moonlight lay all about her as if the world were cocooned in a blanket, tucked in for a good night's sleep. Only she couldn't sleep. Not yet anyway. After an agonizingly long week, they finally had a plan. And more, they had hope. Hope of getting out of Italy and hope of being of service to the War Office. They just had to successfully disguise themselves, enter a gala to which they were not invited in the home of the most prominent trader in Naples, and engage in conversations with enough high ranking gentlemen to acquire knowledge that would be of service to a foreign entity. It all seemed spectacularly challenging and for the first time since boarding that ship in Dover, Kate felt like herself again.

Filled with anticipation for what was to come, Kate suddenly lifted her arms and spun about, her too big skirts twirling in a messy trail behind her. She felt her heart lift as if she were a child again, and the only thing she needed to worry about were which games she would play with her sister that day. She tilted her head back, the moonlight catching her full in the face, and she closed her eyes and spun. She wasn't sure how long she did it, but she suddenly came up against the door leading into the barn, catching herself just as she would have spun into it. She laughed at her own clumsiness, the sound amplified in the quiet of the night.

And then someone was clapping.

She turned, her hands still pressed to the wall of the barn to keep her spinning head from spinning the rest of her over into an ungainly pile on the ground. Thatcher stood in the open doorway to the barn, his face half in shadow as the moonlight only penetrated so far in the space between the house and the barn. But she didn't miss his unmistakable grin, and she turned as quickly as her still foggy head would allow her and presented him her best curtsy.

"Thank you, sir, for your kind acknowledgement. Later, I shall be performing a suite from Pygmalion," she said and lifted her head to smile at him.

She didn't know why she was suddenly feeling so childish. Perhaps the exhilaration of their impending mission was getting the best of her. It was a relief to finally have something to concentrate on, keeping her mind from straying to the cloudy sense of confusion that had fallen over her since meeting Matthew Thatcher.

"You should be on Drury Lane. Your talents are wasted on War Office work," he said.

Kate smiled harder at him. "You're not the first to say such to me, and I'm sure you shan't be the last. But what a scandal! Captain Hadley's daughter treading the boards. My mother would die from the shame."

She walked over to where Thatcher lounged and took a seat on the overturned laundry tub set on the ground beside him. She plopped onto it, the metal protesting with a muffled pop, before propping her head against the barn so she could look up at the night sky, taking in the sea of stars that spread out before her into infinity.

"Would you care so much? About your mother dying from shame?" Thatcher asked.

She tilted her head enough to look up at him as he gazed down at her. "Probably not," she said and was surprised at how quickly the answer came. There was a time when anything only mattered if her mother had given her instruction on it. But it had been years since her mother had given any instruction, to her or her sister, and time had likely worn away its threat. "But what about the plan? Do you think we'll be successful?"

Thatcher adjusted his shoulders against the door jamb, and Kate noticed for the first time the scrapes that crisscrossed his hands. She stood up and without thinking, pulled his hands into hers, being careful not to touch the small cuts.

"What have you been doing, Mr. Thatcher?"

He pulled his hands away almost immediately, and she looked up at him, concern pulling her brow into a crease.

"Just farm work. It happens," he said, and something bristled in the flat tone of his voice. "But will we be successful? I think that depends on what you foresee as success."

Distracted by the discussion of espionage, Kate's mind put the matter of his hands away for a moment to focus on the business at hand.

"The traders will move their cargo if they think a battle is imminent. We should be able to escape on the cargo ships when they leave port. It's unlikely the general's men will search the ships as thoroughly if they believe the ships are only leaving long enough to avoid the fray. We can escape then ," she said, and she felt how large her eyes had grown with the excitement of an impending mission.

Thatcher, however, clearly did not share her excitement, although something appeared to amuse him if his rakish grin was anything to go by.

"But if we are to be of use to the British navy, we must get passage on one of Scevola's ships. They will be the only ones going to Sicily."

Kate nodded. "That will be your job at the masquerade. You must find out if Scevola plans to move his ships."

Thatcher nodded. "While you discover if all the traders plan to move their ships from port and what night."

"Yes," Kate said, "Our plan will only work at the highest moment of confusion. Otherwise, we're likely to get caught."

"Which would help no one," Thatcher concluded.

"We'll get to Sicily, alert the British fleet and be back in time to stop Murat from engaging the Austrian army. If he was foolish enough to engage after the appearance of the British fleet, then he deserves what is coming."

Thatcher raised an eyebrow at her, but she ignored him.

"When we succeed, we will have not only escaped enemy territory but have stopped what could be the most decisive battle for the Italian front in this entire game Napoleon is playing. Can you imagine? I wonder what the War Office will say about Captain Hadley's daughter then !"

She smiled triumphantly at Thatcher, but he was doing

anything but smiling at her. If anything, she would say he was frowning profusely, and it quickly dampened her own joyful mood.

"What is it?"

"You keep saying Captain Hadley's daughter. What about Kate Cavanaugh? What would she think?"

Kate blinked. "I am Kate Cavanaugh," she said, not understanding what he was trying to say to her.

He pushed away from the doorjamb, walking out into the yard to stand closer to her. She thought for a moment he was going to touch her, but he didn't. He stopped less than eighteen inches from her, so close she could smell the scent of soap and wood on him.

"What do you want, Kate?" he asked, and this time his voice carried dimension. She wasn't sure if he was disappointed in her or frustrated, as if he were speaking to a careless child who didn't know better. She didn't care for such an image and quickly took a step back, but he followed her. If she took another step, it would look like she was running away from him, so she stopped where she was, the moonlight she had enjoyed so thoroughly just moments before pressing down on her shoulders like a beacon to Thatcher's accusations.

But as he stared at her, her mind drifted, and she thought of spinning in the moonlight. She thought of the childlike weightlessness that engulfed her if only for a moment.

And so she said, "I'd like to dance."

Thatcher did not say anything nor did he give her one of his raised eyebrows. He only stood in the moonlight with her, the stillness of the night sheltering them from everything else. She almost gave up on him. She almost laughed to ease the tension in the moment, but then he stepped forward, bowing precisely in front of her.

"May I have the honor of this dance, my lady?" he said,

and his drawl was so thick she wanted to bask in the sultry tones until her fingers were prunes.

But instead she returned his bow with her own curtsy, and there in the silence of the night on the ridges above Naples, Kate Cavanaugh danced in the moonlight with Matthew Thatcher, an American she had known for only a few weeks and one with whom she very much feared she was falling in love.

And even though it went against everything she had devoted herself to, she reveled in it.

His hands were rough, much rougher than they had been only days before, and he smelled of sweat and soap and wood, the scents a cacophony of confusion that only bewildered her more than the fact that she was dancing to no music with a man she hardly knew in the middle of a mission gone awry.

But more than that, Thatcher was the right size. For years, she had been plagued with dance partners lacking in vertical prowess but resplendent in horizontal fortitude. It was nice to find his shoulder fit directly under the curve of her hand without her having to drop her arm, and the way his hand fit about her waist, casually and with little effort as they came together.

And then they danced, the only music the sound of the wind passing through the olive trees as the cooler air over the port rushed up into the town and through the ridges to the relative warmth of the farmlands beyond. Kate did not speak and neither did Thatcher. But they watched each other, and although it should have made Kate uneasy, it did not. She felt perfectly at ease dancing, moving to the pulse of a silent song on a darkened hilltop in Naples. She felt perfectly at ease because it was Thatcher, and there was nothing to be afraid of here. With Thatcher there were no rules or guidelines, no expectations or presumption.

Thatcher came with none as far as Kate could tell. There was just a man, a good man, who didn't mind dancing with her no matter how silly it may seem.

Once again, the breathy caress of relief passed through her and over her and for the second time that night, she took note of it. But even as she embraced the exhilaration of it, worry crept up the back of her neck. She hadn't known she needed it. She hadn't known there was anything bothering her enough to feel relief from, and this in itself scared her.

Perhaps Thatcher was right. Perhaps Kate Cavanaugh didn't know what she wanted. Perhaps she only knew what her mother wanted or her father expected. If Kate Cavanaugh was everything she wanted to be why was it such a relief to be who she was when there was no one with weighty expectations watching her?

She stumbled, the thoughts in her mind overcoming the careful steps of her feet, but Thatcher caught her neatly, tipping her back onto the heels of her feet, his grip never tightening. But they had stopped dancing, and now they stood in silence watching each other.

"I don't know what Kate Cavanaugh wants," she finally whispered, Thatcher's soft gaze steady on her face. "I've never asked her."

At the sound of her own words, she felt like a prize idiot, but even as she condemned herself, she knew Thatcher would not.

"I reckon it's time you asked her," he said.

Kate wanted to nod. She wanted to agree with him. She wanted to show some kind of recognition that she had heard him, but there was nothing left of her to think on it. Thatcher still held onto her, one arm about her waist, the other holding her hand. The heat of his body radiated, so close and yet so far away. If only she took a step closer. If only he did so. If only...

"I reckon I should," she whispered, wondering if her voice had disappeared with the rest of her thoughts.

And then Thatcher moved. At the very edge of her sight, she saw his hips move as if he were going to take a step, but then he hesitated. She concentrated on his face, hoping something there would give her a clue as to what he was feeling. The memory of his apology after thoroughly kissing her, only hours old, came rushing back to her in that split second of hesitation. She licked her lips, her mouth going dry at the thought, as she struggled to hope that she had misunderstood him. That he hadn't meant he was sorry he had kissed her, but that he was sorry he had done it so impolitely or some such societal nonsense.

But when he did take a step, it was to step back from her. And then he took another and another after that. Soon he dropped his arms, her own falling to her sides as she stood alone in the moonlight.

"We should get some rest," Thatcher said. "Alberto's wife will be over in the morning to measure us for our costumes."

He wiggled his eyebrows at her, and she thought she was supposed to laugh. But nothing in her felt like laughing just then . His smile faded, and it was just Thatcher standing before her once more.

"I suppose we should," she said, the strength in her voice returning the farther he moved away from her.

"Good night, Kate Cavanaugh," he said, his hand moving to his head as if to tip an invisible cap in her direction.

"Good night, Matthew Thatcher," she said, and then he was gone, leaving her to wonder when it was that being a spy was no longer enough for her.

CHAPTER 8

*H*e looked like a buffoon, and he felt even worse.

Thatcher stood in the front yard of the Salvatores' farmhouse dressed in the costume Mrs. Rossi had created for him out of scraps of fabric Rosa had from years of making clothes for her children and her grandchildren. His jacket was of a fine navy fitted at his waist and accentuated with gold at the lapels and cuffs. His plain black breeches had been commandeered and fitted to his body, tucking nicely into soft black leather boots, the origin of which remained unknown. But they fit well, and he felt himself eyeing them suspiciously from time to time, wondering who the cobbler was who had fashioned them. With the simple gold mask covering his features, he looked simply resplendent, the absolute best he had ever looked. And he hated it.

Waiting for Rosa and Kate to emerge and listening to the sounds of Luigi readying the cart for their transport, he moved from foot to foot, agitation getting the better of him. Whether it was adrenaline brought on by the impending mission or frustration from his uncertainty about Kate, he couldn't be sure. He had undertaken numerous missions for the British War Office and knew this couldn't be a sudden case of nerves.

So if it were not the mission that bothered him, it was Kate. Or rather, his feelings about Kate. He wanted to shuffle his feet in the dirt of the yard, but his boots were too fine to ruin with such childish behavior. He didn't know what to do about Kate, and even as he thought it, his own words came roaring back to him from that night nearly a week before when they had danced in the yard with no music to match their movements. It was likely only the second time in his entire life he employed those ridiculous dance lessons his mama had made him take with Thomas. There was nothing more humiliating than having one's own brother as his dance partner. Thoughts of Thomas brought the usual ache, only now it came with a newer, harder edge to it, and he knew that was because of Kate.

He was falling in love with her.

There was no way around it. The agitation he felt was proof of it. If he kept denying it, he would continue to feel unsettled, but if he admitted it, he didn't know what to do. And even as he reasoned with himself, he realized it didn't matter. He couldn't love Kate, not the way she deserved. He couldn't be there for her. He couldn't be responsible for her. Only once in his life had anyone relied on him for protection, and he had failed in the worst way possible. He had sworn to never let that happen again, and he feared he was getting too close to it with Kate. And it wasn't because she had forced it on him. As she had said herself, circumstances had demanded that they rely on each other in this mission, but that only involved matters of a professional nature. The real Katharine Cavanaugh had no room for a man in her life, even though Thatcher was beginning to suspect it wasn't a matter of not wanting one but not realizing she could want one. Again, it didn't matter because Thatcher was not going to be that man even if she wanted him to be.

But Thatcher had fallen in love with her. He had let her get too close. He had let her matter. And in letting her matter, he put himself in the position of protector, of being responsible for her life, and he hated it. The past burned like a fiery rod in his stomach that no matter how hard he concentrated on something else, he could not make it go away. He had not thought of Thomas so much in the past sixteen years. Thomas haunted him every day, but not like he did now, not with his feelings for Kate so raw and vulnerable.

He would let her down. He knew it. Some basic instinct told him he would fail Kate, and the pain would come back, just as cunning and lethal as it had been that first time when he had seen Thomas slip, when he had watched his hand reach out to catch him before he fell from the ridge. And just as clearly, he saw himself reaching for Kate, his hand grabbing nothing but air. He would fail the person he loved again, and it would be entirely his fault.

"Well, don't you cut a fine figure, Mr. Thatcher?"

He turned at the sound of Kate's voice, finding her standing only a few feet from him in the yard. He hadn't heard her approach and wondered how deeply he had been in his own thoughts to allow her to sneak up on him like that. And then he realized what she was wearing, and his mouth went dry.

When Mrs. Rossi had come to take their measurements, Kate had spoken to the woman in Italian about their costumes, and he had not known anything about what she had in mind. But now he saw it, her vision transformed into a beautiful gown of gold, puckered with spots of deep navy that matched his jacket, and capped at her shoulders, the bodice dipped far too low for his standards. But as a man nonetheless, he enjoyed the display until he realized other men would likely enjoy it as well. He finally let his gaze travel up to her face where a gold mask similar to his hid her features from view.

She looked beautiful. Absolutely beautiful. He wanted to pull her against him and kiss her. Not like he had before, not with such fire and passion. He wanted to kiss her gently, smoothly, softly. He wanted to kiss her with the reverence he felt for her in his heart. He wanted to hold her, his arms stealing around her as if holding a precious treasure. And he didn't want to ever let her go.

And that scared him. One day Katharine Cavanaugh would figure out what she wanted. And what if it didn't include him? Perhaps it would be better for her if it didn't. He would only fail her in the end.

"Thank you," she said, and he blinked up at her.

Her face slid into a mischievous smile as if mocking him.

"You said I looked beautiful," she explained, and he felt heat rise to his face.

"Oh," he said, not realizing he had spoken what was on his mind. He suddenly wondered what else he had said.

She held out her hand. "Would you do me the honor of escorting me to a masked gala, sir?" she said, her tone that of the most prim member of the ton he had ever heard.

The tone didn't fit with the rest of the Kate he knew, and he smiled at her imitation, once more impressed with her ability to slip into a role.

"It would be my honor," he said in turn, scraping a bow at her feet.

He tucked her arm through his and led her over to the cart where Luigi was having some sort of disagreement with the donkey. It was in Italian, so Thatcher wasn't sure what he was saying, but the donkey did not look impressed. Luigi looked up as they approached and finished his conversation with the donkey with a finger pointed in the animal's face. Thatcher raised an eyebrow, but Luigi only smiled at them.

"What a handsome couple it is tonight. We shall be off, then ?" he asked, looking about the yard as a frown made its way onto his face. "Where is the lady of the house?"

Thatcher and Kate both looked back at the house as Rosa emerged, her head for once bare of any kerchief. Her thick black hair with the streaks of gray shimmered in the moonlight, and Thatcher saw for the first time what Luigi must have seen in her those many years ago. She looked like a woman then and not just a person to do the cleaning and the cooking. Thatcher looked back at Luigi to see a smile cross his face.

His eyes were distant as he said, "And that is my wife. You see, she is beautiful."

Thatcher felt the warmth of Kate's arm tucked in his and wondered if he would ever speak those words about someone. It was the first time in his life he had ever even thought of what it would be like to have a wife, and he released Kate's arm almost just as quickly. He helped her into the cart before climbing in behind her. She smiled at him, and he knew it was going to be a long night.

* * *

KATE HAD NOT SEEN the like in any of the ballrooms she had frequented in London or Paris or anywhere else.

Scevola Amoretto's masquerade would outshine any ball any London society matron attempted to host. When Luigi and Rosa had dropped them at a discreet distance from Scevola's home in the hills, there had still been nearly a mile of ground to cover before reaching the residence, and the house glowed like the torch of a lighthouse six inches from the end of her nose. Lanterns were lit along the drive and

around to the promenade that overlooked the port and the
sea beyond. Elegantly dressed ladies and tidily dressed men
streamed into and out of the home as guests made their way
from the ballroom and game rooms inside to the discreet
corners of Scevola's gardens.

She and Thatcher had slipped in through the gardens as
its privacy afforded the most advantage. They strolled up the
stairs from the gardens to the promenade, passing more
sculpture than could be found in the entire country of
Greece. Scevola's money must be very new for it to show
itself so loudly, Kate thought.

The brightness of the ballroom startled her as she had not
expected the place to get any brighter than it already was.
The room was packed with guests costumed in glittering
flourishes and be-feathered masks. She kept her arm tucked
into Thatcher's as he pulled her away into the crush of the
room. She quickly looked about them, but even with her
height, she was no match for seeing over the crowd.

She tugged at Thatcher's arm, pulling his ear closer to her
mouth. "Can you see anything?" she whispered.

He straightened, and she felt him go up on his tip toes.
She looked up to watch him scan the crowd over the heads of
the other partygoers. While he was looking about, she did
her own investigating. It would be up to her to ensure that
enough traders planned to move their cargo out of port on
the night before Murat's attack. They would need adequate
cover to slip out on one of Scevola's ships bound for Sicily.
Only weeks ago, they had had no hope of smuggling themselves out of Naples on a ship, but now, it seemed they would
have the chance. It sent the familiar thrill of anticipation
through her as she felt the end of her mission as if it were a
tangible thing just at her fingertips.

She looked about them and saw many men whose girth
clearly advertised their wealth. Traders were not hurting in

the Kingdom of Naples if the appearance of this ilk were anything to go by. Ladies were dressed in the finest satins and silks with hair swept up with jeweled pins and adorned with fanciful ear bobs and necklaces, hung heavy with gems the colors of rainbows. Even the food looked superb, Scevola clearly wasting no opportunity to proclaim the contents of his coffers to the entire society of Naples.

But would these traders do? Would these traders depend on their livelihood enough to move ships filled with cargo at the sight of a coming battle? Could any of Scevola's ships be easily boarded by a British agent and her trusted mate?

She looked at Thatcher then , thinking him anything but a trusted mate. When she had first seen him in the costume Mrs. Rossi had sewn for him, her heart had simply stopped in her chest. He was gorgeous. But not in the way of cultured men such as the dukes and earls of her acquaintance in London. He was pure man, from the tips of his polished black boots to the wings of his golden mask, he glowed with a sheer maleness that she could never believe existed until she had seen it with her own eyes. His careless curls of golden hair streaked with almost yellow tones from the sun, his skin tanned and smooth from a fresh shave for the first time since she had met him, and his smile, his beautiful wide smile, directed entirely at her. It was almost too much to take.

She looked away and resumed her scan of the room, but not for long as Thatcher tugged on her arm.

"I think Scevola is holding court on the other side of the room," he whispered.

Kate looked in that direction as if she could see through the throng in front of her.

"Can you make it over there?" she whispered in return.

He straightened and looked about the room. "How do you

feel about dancing with musical accompaniment?" he said, his drawl so thick she blinked in response.

"I beg your pardon?"

"Dance with me, Kate," he said, even as his arms moved around her and swung her into the waltz that was already careening across the polished parquet floors of the ballroom.

She clung to him more than followed his lead, his movement so abrupt she had to hang on just to make sure he carried her with him. The music was loud and vibrant, unusual for a waltz, but she felt the beat of it through the floorboards, felt it pull at her insides until her body couldn't help but respond to it. Or perhaps Thatcher was just that good of a dancer. Perhaps she couldn't help but allow him to lead her anywhere.

Sensation shuddered through her at the thought making her look up at his face. For the briefest of moments, she thought it was him. He was the reason the thrill of anticipation was so acute on this mission. But as she felt it, the thought drifted away, and she was left with only the impression of doubt that she had come to know in the past few weeks.

He was tense under her hand, so unlike the Thatcher she had danced with in the moonlight. She looked up at his face again and realized the reason for his tension. He watched Scevola, and even more, he watched everyone around Scevola. Kate had not had adequate opportunities to watch Thatcher attending to his professional duties, and seeing him now reignited the thrill in her. She wondered once more if it were really him that was making everything more exciting on this mission. He was good. He watched everyone without anyone even noticing he was there. He had so skillfully pulled her into the waltz that she was certain no one had seen their entrance, and as such, no one knew they were in the throng of twirling dancers that clogged the floor in the center of the room. And even as they melted into the background, Thatcher watched his target with the acuity of a master.

She wondered briefly if he had expected to be a spy when he grew up. The thought brought a small smile to her lips.

He moved again, and suddenly, they were standing completely still on the opposite side of the room from whence they had started. Her chest heaved with the exertion of a dance that she had always been instructed had a number of sedate qualities. That clearly only applied when one's partner was not Mr. Matthew Thatcher.

He still did not look at her. His gaze riveted on the group of men and women clustered around something in the corner. She presumed that was where Scevola was, but as she still could not see above the crowd, she had to take Thatcher's word for it.

He bent then , his breath a warm caress across her cheek as he said, "We need to make sure he speaks English before you go after your target."

She nodded, her cheek brushing against the wings of his mask.

"Of course," she said. "But how are we to get close enough for us to find out? There's at least twenty people packed around just him. We'll never get through."

Just then the music in the room silenced, and the roar of conversations held at a level necessary to be heard over the music stopped with a suddenness that pulled the very air from the room. Kate's ears rang in the sudden silence, and she looked about her for what had stopped the party.

Looking in the direction that Thatcher had indicated was the court of Scevola, Kate saw a man, a thin man with sunken cheeks, pasty gray with days old stubble that didn't seem to grow. His eyes were sunken and clouded with makeup that seemed to have been applied to give his facial features some depth but only served to make him look more skeletal. His hair was lank and greasy about his head. He wore a suit made entirely of red and adorned with shimmering facets of paste jewels sewn to random places on his person. And he was standing with a foot on each arm of what could only be described as a purple velvet-covered throne. The entire effect was garish, and Kate looked at Thatcher, the question in her eyes. Was this truly Scevola? He shrugged as if to respond.

"Guests, guests!"

Kate looked back at Scevola.

"I welcome you to my home, you friends from near and afar. I welcome all of you noblemen and women, you fearless traders from seas far beyond our own. I welcome you all to celebrate San Gennaro!" he exclaimed in perfect, accented English to a roaring round of applause.

Kate looked at Thatcher. "I have your answer," she said above the din.

Thatcher raised an eyebrow. "And it is?"

"Yes, Scevola, in fact, does speak English."

THATCHER MADE his way through the crowd by sheer physical force. Bodies became more tightly pressed against one another the closer he got to Scevola, and he had to use more force to pry his way through. When he did finally make it to the inner circle, Thatcher could finally see the entire tableau that Scevola created, with himself as the centerpiece. What was obviously a throne plush in purple velvet sat between two servants wielding palm fronds, fanning the place where Scevola had been sitting. Thatcher took a step back when he saw the costumes on the palm-wielding servants. They were men, young it appeared, and dressed only in loincloths, a terrible attempt at Egyptian costume, Thatcher thought. The young men were well muscled, their bare chests solid and contoured, and glistening in the lamplight as they appeared to have been slathered in oil. Thatcher felt his stomach roll and looked away.

Scevola had come down from his dubious perch on his throne and now conversed with a group of men to the far side of the throne. Thatcher noticed that another set of glistening, lightly dressed young male servants was keeping the crowd at bay and only letting in certain people to speak with Scevola. Thatcher eyed the many people pressing in on the space and observed the number of scantily clad females, bosoms heaving at the slightest glance from Scevola as if their person would suddenly break from the garment entirely if Scevola should give them an audience.

But Scevola seemed not to notice the throngs of beautiful women scrambling over each other to get to him. He seemed completely absorbed in the attention of the men he was already speaking to, and just then a memory of what Luigi had said at the kitchen table came slipping back into his mind.

Scevola had unchristian relationships with men.

Looking between the straining women and the men, Thatcher's mind raced with the improbability of the situation. Were the rumors true? Did Scevola prefer company of the decidedly male persuasion?

Thatcher looked behind him as if to ask Kate for her input, but she had already disappeared, off to her own objective of obtaining information about which ships planned to leave Naples. He looked back at the scene in front of him. There was absolutely no way around it. He would need to flirt with Scevola Amoretto if he were to gain any information of value from the man.

He looked down at his horrid costume, suddenly seeing the importance of such garb. He itched with the urge to run his hands over his hair to ensure everything was in the right place. Kate hadn't told him he looked beautiful that evening. He only hoped he did so for the sake of crown and country and his own ass.

He pushed forward, shoving some of the smaller women out of the way until he was within earshot of Scevola and his group of men. They were speaking in English, all parties with heavy accents that led Thatcher to believe that while English was not a first language for any of them, it was a common one, and so they spoke it in order to engage at all with one another.

"Oh, but you surely don't believe him, do you?" Scevola said with an unusual swipe of his hand at one of his companions.

Being closer now, Thatcher saw the age on Scevola's face and wondered how old the man was. At a distance, Thatcher would have guessed him to be no more than thirty years of age, but upon closer examination, he appeared much older, the lines and wrinkles pulling at his face in an unnatural acceleration of time.

"I see no reason not to," said another in the group, making the same motion with his hand back at Scevola.

Thatcher completely expected them to start slapping at each other with all this unnecessary hand waving occurring, but instead, the group burst into a fit of laughter Thatcher could only describe as a fit of the giggles.

"The man had the audacity to claim he had swum from Naples to Sicily! He is delusional if he is not entirely crazy!" Scevola said this with a snort of laughter, and Thatcher took it as his opportunity to interrupt.

"Perhaps a man of lesser abilities than yourself would be deceitful in such a claim, but I can't say I would say the same about you."

He let the drawl run thick through his voice as he slid a

foot forward just far enough to accentuate his torso and the muscles showing through the thin fabric of his breeches. He waited a beat before slowly, very, very, achingly slowly, allowing his mouth to move into a sweet smile.

And he had him.

Thatcher saw the moment Scevola realized who had spoken. The man straightened, his attention bouncing from the group to lock onto Thatcher in a grip that nothing could pry away. One of his companions tried to pull his attention back with what sounded like a pet name followed by a cooing sound, but Scevola had clearly found something much more interesting. He held up a hand as if to stop his companion from speaking and took a step toward Thatcher, his gaze locked on his.

Thatcher's heart raced as he waited for Scevola to do something. He was in entirely unfamiliar, and admittedly uncomfortable, territory, and he could not fail at getting the information he needed to get him and Kate out of Naples.

And then Scevola barked, "Harlow!"

And one of the men holding back the crowd came over and nodded to Thatcher to step forward. He did but only by a step, keeping the distance between him and Scevola teasingly wide.

"You are not from Naples," Scevola said.

"I reckon not," Thatcher said, keeping his drawl thick.

"Would you care for a drink, Mr.--"

"Matthew," Thatcher said, and Scevola smiled.

"Matthew," he said the name as if it were slick with oil and ran from his mouth in a slither. "You come with me, Mr. Matthew."

Scevola turned and walked to the corner of the room where a doorway was hidden behind a curtain of patterned satin. Thatcher looked briefly at the guard Scevola had called

Harlow, wondering for a moment what country he hailed from, before following after the trader.

The doorway led to a corridor lit by a single lantern along the wall. The difference in light had him pausing until his vision adjusted. He saw Scevola strolling down the corridor in front of him and followed, his hips swaying at a ridiculous tilt. The corridor led toward the rear of the house, but Scevola did not travel far before turning off into another room. Thatcher followed carefully, his senses alert to any possible danger. He had not planned to leave the ballroom, and if something befell him now, he wasn't sure Kate could find him. He had to stay sharp.

He stepped into what appeared to be a rather tastefully decorated library. Shelves upon shelves of books lined the perimeter reaching far to the tall ceilings. The floors were covered in conservative carpets, and even the furniture was simple yet tasteful. Thatcher felt an uneasiness growing in the pit of his stomach, but before he could react, he heard the unmistakable sound of a door shutting behind him followed by the distinctive sound of a lock sliding into place. He turned and found Scevola standing in front of the door, his hand still on the knob.

"You're the American they're looking for," Scevola said without preamble, his voice having lost the theatrical lilt it had carried in the ballroom beyond.

CHAPTER 9

*T*hatcher stood there and thought about his options as he let Scevola's words sink in. He was much larger than Scevola and could easily overpower him. But Scevola seemed like the type to have thought of that before leading a strange man into a room alone with him. Lacking all of the information about his whereabouts and the power behind Scevola's forces, the manpower in the ballroom indication enough to give pause, it didn't seem like a wise choice to assault the man. So Thatcher went with his only alternative, which was to get Scevola talking until he could figure something else out.

"Yes, I am," he said. "Who's asking?"

Scevola laughed, the sound natural and unlike any he had emitted in the ballroom. He pulled the key from the lock in the door, depositing it in the pocket of his garish coat.

"You are an interesting person, Mr. Matthew, if that is your name."

Thatcher opened his mouth to respond, but Scevola held up a hand as he circled Thatcher. "Do not tell me your real name. If it is anything else, it is best if you keep it safe with you."

Thatcher looked at him, his sense of uneasiness growing.

"You're not turning me over to the authorities?"

He watched Scevola for any telltale signs of deceit, but the other man just paced around him, until he came to rest with a bent elbow on the back of an upholstered chair, not quite near Thatcher but not quite far away. It was as if he had deflated the moment he had left the ballroom and the need to showcase had dissolved. An ordinary man stood before Thatcher despite the hideous costume and gaunt face.

"Why should I?" Scevola finally said. "It's not as if I have anything to gain from it. But if that should change, I hope you will play nice and come along."

Scevola smiled, and he looked suddenly younger than his ragged features proclaimed. Thatcher felt his sense of unease slip closer to confusion, and he changed his own posturing to signal to Scevola that he was listening.

"What is it you want, American?" Scevola said.

Thatcher hesitated at this. He had to be careful with his next words and not just for himself but for Kate, too. If he failed to obtain the information that Scevola was rumored to have regarding the movement of Murat's men, Thatcher would have failed someone he cared about yet again. If they failed to escape Naples and were caught in the battle, it would be his fault. He thought of Thomas and knew he had to tread wisely.

He had never trained to be a spy and had largely fallen into the profession by accident, the need to earn a wage taking precedent over anything else. Espionage had just been rather lucrative. But no one had ever depended on him to be exceptionally good at it. But now there was a great deal more at stake.

Scevola likely had everything to gain if Murat maintained

control of Naples and likely welcomed the coming battle as long as he could move any of his cargos out of port. If he had been told that Thatcher was a wanted man by the very people that kept him in his position, why wasn't he apprehending him? Scevola shifted, straightening to move to the wall on the far side of the room where a cart had been placed with a decanter of an amber liquor and some glasses. Thatcher watched him pour a finger of the liquid into a glass and hold it up to Thatcher.

"Drink, American? It's fine French brandy," he smiled at these words. "I understand some other nations may miss such exquisite niceties." He said this last part with a knowing wink.

Thatcher cleared his throat and shook his head.

Scevola's smile faded slowly, and he said, "You and your lady friend, the one in the gold dress, what is it you seek?"

Thatcher went cold. It moved in a wave from his feet, through his legs, past his torso and into his face. Scevola knew about Kate. More specifically, he knew about Kate in that moment, just beyond the walls of the room, searching through the crowd for local merchants to give her information they needed to escape. He took an involuntary step forward, not sure what he intended to do, but the instinct to protect Kate surged through him with physical force. He had to do something, but Scevola held up a hand again.

"She will not be harmed, I assure you," he said, but Thatcher trusted that about as much as he trusted his own ability to protect her. "I have no game to play with you, American, but I do know you were not on my guest list. So you must come here for a reason. What is it?"

Thatcher swallowed, deciding he must lay bare at least some of his intentions if he had any chance of saving Kate, of getting her on a ship out of Naples and safely to the British navy in Sicily.

"We need information about the pending battle with the Austrians. We need to know for certain when Murat plans to attack."

Scevola did not hesitate. "For what purpose? Are you and your lovely friend going to stop him all by yourselves?"

"We hope to gain passage on one of the trading ships when they move out of port to protect their cargos. We wish to gain passage to Sicily."

Scevola did not respond at first. He took a sip of his drink as he watched Thatcher with unfeeling eyes.

"Gain passage? You mean smuggle yourselves out in the cargo bay," Scevola said with a bland tone.

Thatcher reluctantly nodded, unsure as to how the merchant in front of him felt about stowaways. He thought Scevola would stop speaking then , as his face remained passive, not even the sarcastic smile returning to his features.

Until finally, he said, "I cannot help you, American. I wish that I could."

Scevola finished the last of his drink and carefully set the glass on the cart. Thatcher took another step closer to him.

"Please, Mr. Amoretto, my friend, the woman in the gold dress, she's--"

Scevola held up that hand again. "Please do not tell me of some unrequited love affair, Mr. Matthew. I cannot be bothered with such things," he said.

Thatcher blinked in confusion. "That's not it at all, Mr. Amoretto," he said, but at the sudden look of interest on Scevola's face, Thatcher felt the words stop in his throat.

Scevola looked at him as a starving man looked at a rump roast. Thatcher retreated a small step, a movement of his feet more than an actual retreat. Scevola made up for the distance by taking several paces towards him. The man came so close Thatcher detected the unmistakable scent of a powerful citrus cologne, not at all intriguing or appealing. Thatcher wanted to take another step back.

"That's not it?" Scevola said, the coaxing smile returning to his face. "Then what is it, exactly?"

Scevola reached out a hand, one slim finger, the nail long and filed to a delicate point, extended. That single finger reached the cuff of Thatcher's jacket, running in the barest of touches along the seam before falling away. Thatcher's stomach heaved, and he forced the image of Kate, twirling in the moonlight to push out the feeling of revulsion that swept through him at Scevola's touch.

Scevola must have read something in his face, because he turned away, heading in the direction of the door.

"It is not that I do not wish to help you, American. It is that I can't," Scevola said, and Thatcher watched as he pulled the key to the lock from his pocket.

Staring at the key, Thatcher once again felt a cold wave pass through his body as Scevola's words registered. He couldn't help them? Desperation flooded his senses, and he forced himself to remain focused, to stay on target. Kate depended on him.

"Why not?" Thatcher asked, following Scevola in the direction of the door, refusing to allow the man to retreat from him.

Scevola turned, and Thatcher saw him momentarily back up as if he were surprised that Thatcher was so close. Thatcher got as close as he dared to the other man, the blood pounding in his temples as he realized he was failing her, failing Kate. He had sworn never to let this happen. He swore to never fail another person who depended on him again. But then , he had sworn to never allow someone to get that close to him, and he failed at that as well. The feeling of impossible failure swept through him with the same strength that had driven him from his family's plantation sixteen years before when he had not saved his brother. The sensation was terrifying in its strength and thrilling in its power. He needed an answer from Scevola, and he wasn't leaving until he got it.

He wasn't sure what reflected on his face, but whatever it was, it had Scevola backing up again, backing up and talking.

"Because there is to be no battle," Scevola said quietly, his eyes wide as he studied Thatcher. "I am sorry, American, but Murat has moved his forces to Tolentino. He will strike there on the first of May."

Thatcher's heart stopped, the adrenaline surging through his veins arrested in its place.

"The cargo ships--"

"Will not be moved as they are in no danger where they are."

Thatcher took two steps forward now, his only thoughts that of Kate twirling in the moonlight, Kate spooning gobs of pasta into her mouth, Kate standing in her golden dress in the twilight. Kate. He felt desperation replace the adrenaline.

"Please, sir, perhaps you can give us--"

"I have nothing to gain by turning you in, but I do have everything to lose if I help you." He paused then , his face changing as if an idea had suddenly come to mind. He extended a hand again, that same thin finger with the too long nail reaching toward Thatcher, caressing the cuff of his jacket before pulling away. Scevola looked up at him through his lashes in much the same way many a damsel would. "Unless, of course, you are looking for new employment. I would be happy to offer assistance in exchange for you assuming a post on my staff."

He thought Scevola wasn't being serious until the man looked at him fully, his face as serious as anything. Thatcher felt his skin crawl and jerked his arm out of Scevola's reach.

"I'm sorry," Thatcher said, "It's not--"

Scevola waved him off again. "I understand, but I had to try for someone as handsome as you."

Scevola turned and inserted the key in the lock, turning it with a decisive click. He pulled the door open with a soft swoosh and paused as if waiting for Thatcher to step through it.

Thatcher did not move at first, but finally, he managed a step and then another.

"American," Scevola called to him when he had stepped into the corridor.

Thatcher stopped and turned to look at him.

"Don't forget about my offer if you find yourself with no hope," he said and quietly shut the door in Thatcher's face.

* * *

KATE SAT in the knotted grasses of the hills surrounding Naples, heedless of what it was doing to her beautiful golden dress. The night had cooled, and the breeze carried a chill. But after the intense heat of the overcrowded ballroom, the cool caress was welcomed. She carried no shawl and, except for her white gloves and the caps of her sleeves, her arms were bared to the night air, and she watched as her skin prickled at the coldness. But she didn't notice its bite. She stared up at the stars that only a few nights ago had held such promise. Promise of escape. Promise of fulfillment. Promise of living up to every expectation anyone could have for the daughter of Captain Hadley.

But as soon as Thatcher had found her in the ballroom, as soon as she had seen the look on his face, the set of his mouth, the fear in his eyes behind his golden mask, she knew they had failed. She knew just by looking at him that all was lost. Their glorious plan had not found success.

They were trapped.

Thatcher had not said anything then . He had simply taken her arm and led her back onto the promenade and out into the gardens. They slipped away just as quickly as they had come, and the night swallowed them with welcoming arms. They had traveled for several miles in the direction of Luigi's farm until finally, Thatcher had pulled her off the road, stepping into the deep wild grasses along the pass. He sat next to her now, his arms dangling over his bent knees, his gold mask long discarded to be shoved into the pocket of his jacket. She handed him her own mask now, carefully unpinning it from her hair and handing it to him. He took it without a word and shoved it into the same pocket to join the other one.

His explanation of what had happened with Scevola had been succinct and without emotion, but Kate knew Thatcher burned with feelings he did not proclaim. He didn't tell her what it was, and she didn't ask him to explain. She only allowed the information he conveyed to seep into her senses like mist after a rain seeping through her clothes without her realizing it.

Murat and his men were not coming to Naples. She should have known it would be too easy. She should have known that it was all too easy. She should have known that it could not have been as simple as making their way onto a merchant vessel, escaping during the chaos of battle. She should have known. She could almost hear her mother's condescending tone, scolding her for her carelessness, but even as she heard it, she pushed it away on the night breeze, not caring for the maternal words in the least.

Finally, she looked at Thatcher to find him studying the tops of his boots in the tall grass. He was not a man to fidget, and Kate watched as the stillness grew about him, leaving no clue as to his thoughts to the casual observer. But Kate knew better. Kate knew Thatcher better. So she elbowed him, a gentle poke in his side. He looked at her, and she smiled. But Thatcher only returned his gaze to his boots.

"Oh, come now, it's not all that bad," she said, but Thatcher did not respond.

She looked out to the sea and for the first time, noticed the lights in the port, noticed the movement of people, which from their vantage looked like little swarms of ants moving about in some kind of random fashion.

"Look," Kate said, hoping to distract Thatcher. She had never worked with an agent who took an unfulfilled objective so hard. "The festival in the port. Perhaps we could make our way down there and join them," she said with a half-hearted laugh.

She turned to Thatcher to see if he was laughing, too, but he only stared at her. In his eyes, she saw pain, a real pain, like none she had seen before. Her throat closed at the sight of it, her hand going to her chest in an involuntary response to his ache.

"Thatcher, what is it?" she asked.

"I've let you down," he said, his voice not more than a whisper.

At first she thought she had heard him wrong, but then he said, "I'm sorry, Kate. I tried to get Scevola to help us. I tried to get him to give us passage on one of his ships--"

"What?" she interrupted, his words coming faster than she could process them. "You asked Scevola for help? What if he tells the general? You said Scevola told you they were looking for us. If Scevola tells the authorities that we asked to be smuggled out on a ship, the general is sure to order his men to search every vessel very carefully."

"Scevola won't tell," Thatcher said, his words neutral and soft. His very tone sent a shiver down her spine.

"How do you know that?" she asked.

"Because he has nothing to gain from it," Thatcher said, his gaze moving out to the port and the sea beyond.

"Thatcher, you didn't fail me," she said then , hoping to draw him back to his revealing words. That would explain his dismal appearance. It was one thing to have no hope of escape, but it was another to think you had failed another. "Thatcher," she prompted when he did not speak.

"I had a little brother," he said, and at first, Kate thought he was avoiding the topic, but then he looked at her, his gaze so intense, she girded herself for what was to come. "His name was Thomas. He was born when I was almost nine years old, so I always felt I had to take care of him. It was my duty, you know?"

He paused here, his gaze seeming to drift through her, but she knew he didn't seek a response. His use of the past tense when he referred to Thomas sent a chill over her arms that had nothing to do with the cool night breeze.

"What happened to Thomas?" she asked, prodding even though she suspected she needn't have. But there was something about him that begged her to interact, that begged to engage in whatever it was that Thatcher needed to say. It was almost as if he had wanted to have this conversation forever, but there had been no one there to listen. Only she was there now, and she listened.

"Thomas died," Thatcher said, his gaze never leaving the indistinguishable line of the horizon. "I wanted to try a new fishing hole. It was in a ravine, and my father told me I wasn't to go there because it was dangerous. But I never really listened when I was that age. I was young, and I could do anything. So I went, and Thomas followed me. He slipped on the way down. I couldn't catch him. He was only eight years old."

He relayed the entire story with such detachment, it had Kate's stomach clenching. Thatcher must have been sixteen at the time. Sixteen was such a delicate age. What had it taken for such a young man to recover from that? From not saving his own little brother?

"I left," Thatcher said. "I just left. I couldn't be there anymore knowing what had happened. Knowing what I had let happen."

"Oh, Thatcher," she said, as she struggled with everything he said, the enormity of it falling about her like leaves falling from a tree in fall, their touch gentle in their reminder that change is sweeping.

"My father didn't want me to go. I was supposed to take over the running of the plantation from him. I was going to be a man soon. He wanted me to step into his shoes. But I couldn't stay there. I couldn't be in a place with so many memories of Thomas. So many reminders of how I had failed."

Kate's mind reeled as everything fell into place. Thatcher's abhorrence of the farm. Thatcher's reaction to her explanation about her father's expectations. Thatcher's black mood at relaying the information that would keep them trapped in Naples.

"It's not your fault," she heard herself say before she had really figured it all out. "It's not your fault, Thatcher."

She didn't know what she was telling him wasn't his fault. The lack of battle to rescue them from the port or the death of his brother. Whichever it was, she had to make sure he knew that it was true.

"I didn't protect him," Thatcher said, and the strain in his voice was apparent.

Kate reached out, her hand cupping his cheek, feeling the smoothness of his skin against the palm of her hand.

"It wasn't your fault, Thatcher. You made a poor, careless choice, but you were a child. You're an adult now, and you can make sure it never happens again. When a choice presents itself, you have the power to make the right one."

Something shifted in his eyes. She wasn't sure if it was her touch or her words that did it, but suddenly, he softened. He reached for her, and she let him take her.

* * *

HE ABSORBED her kiss like a man starved for it. He hadn't known he was reaching for her until the warmth of her skin moved under his fingertips, sliding through his touch until his lips met hers. He cradled her head in his hands, angling his own to match the depth of her kiss, to push it further. She tasted of goodness and heat, promise and desire. She tasted like everything he had imagined she would.

He moved into her, lying her back into the softness of the wild grass. It enveloped them, shielding them from everything else, the hillside, the port, the night and everything that had occurred in it. In that moment, it was just him and Kate, alone together. He nibbled at the corners of her mouth, slipped his tongue along the seam of her lips. She moaned her pleasure as her hands threaded through his hair. He surged with desire at the feel of her nails scraping along his back through his jacket.

He sat up long enough to shed his jacket, wanting to feel more of her touch. He trailed kisses along her brow, the line of her jaw and down her neck, resting his lips on the tantalizing beat of her pulse. She squirmed beneath him, and he dared to take a nip at her throat. She jerked against him, her hands stilling on his back at the same time her nails dug into him as she held on. He smiled against her throat, kissing the skin he had just offended.

"Thatcher," she said, her voice strained and not entirely her own.

He moved lower, finding the delicate edge of her collar bone even as his hands worked at the edge of her bodice, moving the fabric, so he could trace a single fingertip along the rim of her bosom, as much as the dress would allow. It wasn't enough, and he moved his hands to the back of her gown, lifting her slightly off the ground as his fingers quickly searched for buttons to undo, to give him access to what he wanted. He found them, a small trail of buttons down her back. His big fingers slipped on them, but he managed enough to slip one sleeve off her shoulder, baring her to him. A thin chemise was all that remained between her bare skin and his touch. He stopped for a moment, picking his head up to look at her.

Her eyes were closed, her head thrown back, the line of her throat a pale swath of skin. He wanted to kiss her there again, but his gaze traveled farther, moving down the tender line of her neck to where it slipped into the contours of her chest and then to the revealing qualities of her chemise. Her dark aureoles showed through the thin fabric. He could clearly see the outline of her breasts, and he stared at them, never realizing until that moment just how beautiful she was. In the whole time he looked at her, she did not open her eyes. She lay in the grass, resplendent in her beauty as the light of the stars and moon bathed her in an ethereal glow that only made him want her more.

He dipped his head, his tongue encircling the dark shape of her nipple through her undergarment. She bucked beneath him, her hands coming up to grab his head. Whether she tried to push him away or pull him closer, he wasn't sure, but he sucked at her nipple, lapped at it with his tongue, until she squirmed violently beneath him.

"Thatcher, please," she said, and he smiled now, reaching up to push the strap of the chemise over her shoulder. The garment fell away, revealing just the smallest bit more of her skin, the swell of her breast. He nuzzled it, moving his lips along the line of her chemise as he pushed it down with each kiss. Finally, he exposed her nipple, swollen and pebbled from his touch. He brought it into his mouth, sucking softly as one hand reached down, pulling up the length of her skirt.

Her legs fell apart for him as if drawing him into her body. He settled between them as his fingertips found the lace of her garter, the ties of her stockings. He thought for a moment about undoing one of the ties, releasing the stocking to trail down her leg, baring it to him. But there was something far more erotic in allowing her stockings to remain in place even as he lifted her skirts to her hips.

He sat back on his heels to take in all of her. She lay before him, a woman lost in her own desire. He trailed his gaze along her hair, now released of its pins and twining in the leaves of the grass, her one bared breast, a lustrous pearl in the moonlight, her legs spread wide for him, the white of her silk stockings ending in the pale, forbidden flesh at the top of her thighs. It was all there before him, waiting for him to take her.

He leaned over her, pressed a kiss to the sensitive spot behind her ear.

"Kate," he said, his voice unexpectedly strained. He wanted to be inside of her. He had to be inside of her and soon. There was an urgency to the moment like he had never felt before. There was something he couldn't quite grasp. Perhaps it was something about his love for her. He had never loved another before, had never felt for anyone the things he felt for Kate. Maybe that's what made this different now. Maybe that's what made the tastes sharper, the feelings more acute, the need more fierce.

"Kate, tell me it's all right," he said, his words whispered against her ear.

She responded with a mewling sound, but he pushed forward, needing to her say it.

"Kate, I need you to open your eyes. I need you to tell me."

She writhed beneath him, her head rocking back and forth in the grass, her silky hair caressing his cheek. He turned for a moment, burying his face in the thick tresses, smelling the hint of soap and lavender.

"Kate," he said again, lending an edge to his tone.

Finally, she opened her eyes, her gaze traveling to the stars beyond them.

"Look at me, Kate," he said, and he took her chin in his hand, gently tugging until he saw her eyes fixed on him. "Tell me you want this, Kate."

She licked her lips, and he almost lost himself. But he swallowed, hard, and waited.

"Kate, I need to know this is all right. I need to know that you want this, too. If you don't, I'll just stop now."

He didn't trust his own words and wondered why he had even said them. He couldn't stop now. There was nothing that could stop him.

"Yes," she said. The word was soft, almost a breath more than a word, but he heard it.

He surged up, his hands flying to the fastenings of his breeches, pulling them loose and down, freeing his throbbing erection. He leaned over her, careful to keep his weight off of her. He caressed the silken skin at her opening, his fingers finding her damp warmth. He prodded her folds, watched her face to see which of his touches she liked. She bit her lower lip, and he suspected she liked all of his touches. He smiled, his fingers moving knowingly to her sensitive nub. He flicked a single finger over it, and she spasmed, her hips coming off the ground, driving her into his hand.

"Thatcher!" she screamed, and her eyes flew open.

He needed her. And he needed her now. He prodded her

with the tip of his penis, feeling the damp as he slid against her. With two fingers, he separated her folds, finding her opening wet for him. Without another thought, he drove into her, nearly sinking to the hilt.

But when Kate screamed, he knew it was not a sound of pleasure. He froze, the unmistakable tightness of her sheath, the moment of resistance as he buried himself in her, her now frantic movements to get away from him.

"Kate, stop moving," he said through gritted teeth. "For God's sake, just stop moving."

But she continued to move, squirming as she tried to get away from him.

"Thatcher, please," she said, her voice filled with pain and tears, and he had never felt worse in his life.

"Kate," he said, but it was too late. He came, the feeling of relief so intense he crumbled with it. He hastily pulled out of her, rolling off of her and into the grass. He lay there as his heart thundered and his chest heaved. He lay there as he listened to the sounds of Kate's muted whimpers. When he thought he had control of himself again, he moved, pulling Kate into his arms, putting a finger under her chin to lift her gaze to his.

When she finally looked at him, he said, "How in the hell are you still a virgin?"

CHAPTER 10

"**B**ut I am a virgin," Kate said, wanting to look anywhere but at Thatcher. "Or was," she corrected weakly.

He wouldn't let her move her head though, his grip on her chin unrelenting, and so she stared into his bright blue gaze.

"I gathered as much," Thatcher said, and she felt her face flame in embarrassment. "But how is it that a woman such as yourself, being of your acquired age, is still a virgin?"

Kate's face flamed hotter. "I told you. I had no use for a man in my life. My objective--"

"Jesus Christ," Thatcher said, and now she did look at him, shocked by his sudden use of blasphemy. "I didn't think that meant you abstained entirely from the act."

She struggled against his arms, not wanting to have this conversation lying down, but he wouldn't release his grip on her.

"I don't take such matters lightly, Mr. Thatcher," she said, falling back against him as she gave up struggling. "I've never been with a man." She hesitated. "Before tonight."

Thatcher's eyes were intense on her, studying every facet

of her face. She wanted to squirm, feeling the heat of accusation in his gaze alone.

She should have stopped him. She should have said something. He had even asked her. He had given her a moment to think about it, to think about what was happening. He had waited for her response, prodded her for it, pushed for it, before he had done anything. This was entirely her fault. She may have been a virgin, but she knew what Thatcher was doing. She knew what they were doing.

Never had she been so reckless. Never had she been so careless. By all accounts, she was now a ruined woman. If it weren't for her cover as a widow, she would be dismissed by society.

But it was worse than that, because she had wanted Matthew Thatcher to make love to her. In the moment of his deepest pain, something in her resonated with a matching pulse. She felt for him, felt his anguish, and deep within her felt the resounding call of her own confusion. There was so much that Thatcher carried inside of himself and for an instant, she wanted it all to go away. She wanted the confusion she had carried with her these past few weeks to lift. She wanted the pain in his face to disappear. She wanted it to be only about Kate and Thatcher for just a few minutes.

And it had been. And it had been glorious up until that last bit, but she suspected that was her fault. She should have told Thatcher she was a virgin.

But now she couldn't look at him. Now she was once more engulfed in the confusion she had tried so hard to push away. She was a spy for the War Office. That was what she had told herself since the day she knew she would carry on her father's legacy at the Office. And in the ten years since assuming her position, nothing had ever threatened her devotion to her duty. But now it did and in the most spectacular way possible.

Katharine Cavanaugh had just taken a lover.

And because she wasn't looking at him, she didn't see his kiss coming until his warm lips were on hers. It startled her, as she could not imagine him wanting to kiss her again for the rest of his life. She had deceived him, a terrible transgression that she could have prevented. He kissed her with abandon, and the low throb deep in her stomach, the burning ache that had fled the moment he had entered her, flared back to life. She felt it surge up, her body moving against his as if she wanted more. But she didn't want more. The entire act had been lovely, but the finale had been deplorable, filled with pain at the worst of it and terrible discomfort at the best. And yet her body was responding in a way she could not control. Her dress still hung off one shoulder, and her bared chest pressed against the fabric of his shirt. She felt her nipples tighten in response, and the tension in her stomach moved lower, the burning ache growing.

But when his hand touched the skin at the top of her thigh, she jerked away, severing their kiss.

"Easy," Thatcher said, his eyes fluttering open as she looked up at him. "I'm not going to hurt you again. I wouldn't have hurt you the first time had I known."

The first time? Was there to be a second time? She most certainly hoped not.

"I don't want that to be the only thing you know about love making," he said, his gaze intent on her face, watching for what she didn't know, so she let her expression remain vague, the only emotion she had strength left to feel. "I want you to know the pleasure of it. I want you to know that it can be very good if both parties are honest and open with each other."

His last words were heavy with meaning, and regret swamped her.

"I'm sorry, Thatcher," she said finally, but he cut off any more apology as he kissed her again.

The hand at her thigh moved higher, and his fingertips brushed over the most intimate part of her. She jerked away involuntarily, the skin there still sore from its earlier encounter with the most intimate parts of Thatcher. But he didn't retreat. He kept his hand there, pushing gently, stroking and caressing. Slowly, the skin there began to tingle, and she felt an odd sense of gathering that she couldn't name. It was more intense than it had been before, and she yearned for a fulfillment she didn't understand.

"Thatcher," she groaned, pulling her lips from his as she struggled to breathe.

It was all becoming more than she could bear, much like it had before, only now she felt like she was moving toward something, as if there was a finish approaching that she must accomplish above all else. And then Thatcher slipped one finger inside of her. The muscles of her body reacted without her knowing, tightening around the intrusion as fear that he would try to enter her again swept through her. Her eyes flew open, but Thatcher only grinned at her.

"Not any more of that tonight," he said. "This is only about you now."

She didn't know what that meant, but his words calmed her. Her eyes slid shut as she let herself drift back into the pleasure his finger stroked inside of her. She felt the ache progressing, felt the burning grow. And then another finger touched the sensitive nub above her folds. She jerked again, but now she clung to him, not pushing him away in the least. His finger circled her at the same time the other one inside of her stroked at her. He slid the finger in and out, slowly and deliberately as his other finger kept up the constant circles around her nub. He didn't change the rhythm or direction, and soon it was driving her mad.

"Thatcher," she said uselessly, knowing she needed him to do something but not what it was.

"It's all right, Kate," he said, his lips suddenly at her ear, his mouth moving in a searing line along her jaw.

And then his fingers changed their assault. He withdrew his finger from her sheath and concentrated on her sensitive nub, his rhythm picking up pace. Her hips began to move against his hand without her control. The ache gathered to a point, and she pushed against it, knowing there must be more. And then everything exploded. She would have screamed, but Thatcher's mouth came down on hers just as the sensation rocketed through her body, undulating in waves through her limbs. The shock of it pulsed long after Thatcher stopped touching her, long after he had once more gathered her into his arms, cradling her head on his shoulder, stroking a hand through her hair.

She lay there, feeling her breath evening out, her body relaxing into a stupor so deep, she had never felt the like before. She heard the beat of Thatcher's heart beneath her ear, surprised at its rapid pace. Had her pleasure affected him so? Had giving her pleasure driven him to such a physical reaction? Her eyes fluttered open, looking down the length of him to where his pants remained unfastened. He had adjusted himself though, and she could no longer see his manhood, only the dissemble of the opened breeches. For a moment, she regretted not looking earlier. She had been so consumed that she had missed the opportunity to see him naked. Lying there, sated, she hoped she would have the opportunity again.

But Thatcher was oddly still beneath her now, his hand no longer stroking her hair but resting at the nape of her neck. She wanted to ask him what he was thinking. But as the night air moved against her, cooling her heated flesh, the only sound the sound of their breathing and the wind in the reeds of grass, she didn't want to speak. She didn't want to ruin this unexpected moment of tranquility in an otherwise unpredictable situation.

They had failed in their mission that night. They were trapped in Naples, and battle was coming to the north. But that was not the worst of her sins that night. For the first time in her life, Katharine Cavanaugh cared about something other than her duty as an agent.

And as she let her eyes fall shut, as she let her body relax, she thought her body betrayed her, committing the greatest sin of the night. She thought she told Thatcher she loved him.

* * *

MAY WAS QUICKLY APPROACHING, and with it, Murat's attack at Tolentino. The city was far north of the Kingdom of Naples, and Thatcher thought it unlikely that any of the direct fighting would make its way south. But he felt the urgency of it like he had not felt anything before then.

Katharine Cavanaugh loved him.

She had said as much as she had fallen asleep against him on the hillside above the port, the stars and the moonlight the only other witnesses to her declaration. Her words had been the final catalyst that had spurred the decision he had already made and had only yet to admit. He had to get Kate out of Naples no matter the cost. He couldn't lose her, not like he had lost Thomas. There was nothing he wouldn't sacrifice to get her to the safety of Sicily.

Nothing.

It was several days past their ill-fated mission when Thatcher had the opportunity to steal away. He had wanted to go sooner, the very day after Kate declared her love for him, but the opportunity had not come up until then . He had waited, his patience thin, until the right moment when Luigi believed he was helping Rosa with something in the house, and Rosa and Kate believed he was out in the fields with Luigi.

He had left early, taking most of an hour to get across the slopes of the hillsides to Scevola's house without being seen. He was careful not to take the same route back after he finished with the necessary business. He had returned just before the noon meal, dusty and disheveled from his discreet journey through the hills, but it had been worth it. An agreement had been struck, and Kate would soon be out of Naples and safely on her way to Sicily. That was all that mattered.

He wanted to tell her first and alone. He wanted to ensure she understood what was to happen. Kate had an unusual way of responding to a situation with demands for instructions and the possibilities of obtaining valuable information for the War Office. It was natural when one considered her devotion to her position as an agent and her engrained ability to act in that direction. He didn't want to hold such a conversation in front of Luigi and Rosa. They already knew too much, and it would not do to put more weight on their already bowed shoulders.

He went to the kitchen window and peered in. Kate stood alone at the table, her hands deep in a bowl of what appeared to be dough. Rosa was nowhere to be seen. He tapped lightly on the window until she looked up. He was struck by her beauty as he always was, the quick smile that came to her full mouth when she saw him. He gestured toward the barn, and she frowned at him, holding up her floury hands and rolling her eyes at him. He looked about and saw Rosa making her very slow way up the hill to call in Luigi for the noon meal. He figured there may be enough time.

The kitchen was dark and cool when he entered it, the room full of aromas so vibrant he thought he could reach out and touch them. Kate turned her head toward him as he came in, her smile once more on her face. He wanted to kiss her. He wanted to wrap his arms around her and pull her against him. But as they had done all week, they avoided contact when not in the confines of their stalls in the barn. Such engagement was neither prudent nor wise, so he stepped around her, putting the table between them.

"I've bartered passage out of Naples on a merchant vessel leaving port tomorrow night," he said without preamble.

Kate jumped, knocking the bowl of dough nearly off the table. He caught it before it could go over the edge and shatter on the floor. He righted it, his eyes remaining fixed on the pottery longer than was necessary. He suddenly realized he didn't want to see the look in Kate's eyes. He didn't want to see the joy on her face, the elation of rescue. Because it wouldn't be real or deserved, because he wouldn't tell her the truth, or at least not the whole truth. He would not tell her what cost he had to pay for her safety.

"What?" she said finally, and he looked up at her.

Her expression was much as he had expected it would be. Her eyes were alight with anticipation, and he could sense the wheels in her head spinning, moving ahead to the plan that such an announcement obviously required. Her joy was palatable, and he hated all of it. But the only thing that mattered was to make sure she was safe.

"I've secured passage out of Naples. A merchant vessel is to leave port tomorrow night for Sicily. You will be on it, Kate," he said, unable to simply say that he had gained them passage on a ship. The lie became stuck in his throat as soon as he thought of it. It was best if he said as little as possible.

And then Kate's hands came out of the bowl of dough, and she raced at him. She kept her arms up, locking them around his neck to prevent flour from getting all over his clothes. But she rested her body against his as if to hug him.

His heart stuttered in his chest, but his arms came around her without pause, anchoring her to him. He felt her shudder against him, and he pushed his head back far enough to realize she was laughing. Her laugh came out in great hiccups, and her eyes were squeezed shut as if the joy were too much.

He stood there watching her, the absolute epitome of happiness, and he fell in love with Katharine Cavanaugh.

And he wanted to die.

He had already died at the moment he realized he loved her completely. He was going to break her heart. He had to break her heart. It was the only way he could make sure she was safe. He wouldn't make a mistake this time. He wouldn't let someone else he loved so much meet such a tragic end. He wouldn't survive it. But he wouldn't survive this either. He wouldn't survive what he had to do.

He was still holding her when Rosa and Luigi entered the kitchen on a stream of Italian, Rosa's hands moving in the air as if directing a symphony orchestra. They stopped at the sight of them, and Thatcher felt as if he were caught with his hand up a girl's dress at school. But Kate turned about, her floury hands still in the air, fingers spread wide, and proclaimed, "Thatcher has secured passage for us on a ship out of Naples!"

She said this in English, and Thatcher assumed Luigi repeated it in Italian as he turned swiftly to Rosa. And then Luigi was hugging him, the smaller man only coming up to the middle of Thatcher's chest. Slowly, Thatcher put his arms around him, returning the embrace as best he could. His mind wandered to what it had been like to hug his own father as a boy, to feel the security of his father's arms. And for a moment, a moment so brief he might have missed it, but so unusual that he was sure he could not have, Thatcher wondered what it would have been like if he had stayed. He wondered if his father would have continued to embrace him after Thomas' death. But as he had not stayed, Thatcher pushed the thought from his mind, his thoughts careening back to the present and the feel of a small Italian man embracing him with simple and pure joy.

Only then did Thatcher become aware of the silence in the room, of Luigi pulling away from him. He looked over to see Rosa had not moved. She stood just inside the kitchen, her hands frozen in front of her as she had been in the middle of speaking when she had entered to find Kate in Thatcher's arms. Thatcher had expected the woman to be joyful or, at the least, happy with the announcement, but her face remained a mask of confusion and perhaps pain.

Thatcher looked to Kate for explanation and saw the same look of confusion on her face. Kate only shook her head. It was Luigi who stepped forward, taking Rosa's frozen hands into his own, his Italian filtered with tones of comfort. Thatcher stepped closer to Kate, wanting to put an arm around her and knowing he could not. Rosa finally said something to Luigi, and Kate shook her head.

"What is it?" Thatcher asked.

Kate's voice was strained when she replied, "She doesn't want to leave their home."

* * *

KATE WATCHED Rosa as silent tears made their way down the older woman's softened cheeks. The woman did not sob or cry out. She did not shake with the heartache. She simply stood there, the sadness rolling off of her in waves that Kate felt to her very core.

The sadness resonated with her in a way Kate had not expected. Rosa looked about her, at the walls, at the furniture, at the pots of water boiling on the stove. This was her home. This was where she had raised her children and then her grandchildren. This was all she had ever known. The walls held the tales of boyish games while the floors held the footsteps of spoiled grandchildren. Rosa told Luigi that she could not leave it all behind now. She could not leave the only thing that she had that told her she had raised a family, that told her she had fulfilled her duties as a mother and a wife.

Kate felt something on her cheeks and was surprised when she wiped away tears. She stood there in the kitchen of an Italian woman she had only met weeks earlier and cried for the loss she was about to endure because of power hungry men that she would never meet. The injustice was more than Kate could bear, and she stood there, letting the tears run down her cheeks.

But Luigi took Rosa's shoulders in his hands, soothing her with his touch. She gestured toward her kitchen, asking him what would happen to her mother's pots and her grand-mother's pottery. Her mother had made bread in those pans for sixty years and Rosa for over forty. What was to happen to them? Who would make bread with them now?

Luigi tried to tell her that it didn't matter. That these were all things that they would replace when they got to Sicily. Their sons were there. Their sons would take care of them. Nothing mattered beyond that. But Rosa could not be consoled. Her eyes continued to travel about the room as if cataloging all of the things she was about to lose. When she still did not look at him, Luigi shook her gently. Her eyes snapped to his, and Kate thought she would rail at him. But when her eyes focused, the older woman stopped talking, silence falling over her like a veil at the mere sight of her husband standing before her.

Luigi told her that Angelo, Paulo, and Bruno needed her. Maria, Adelina, and Doretea needed her help to take care of all of them. Their family needed them, even their little grandchildren. Kate smiled at this, knowing their youngest grandchild was sixteen years of age. Rosa seemed to melt in front of her, and she began to cry in earnest. Luigi pulled her against him, his arms wrapping tightly about her shaking form.

Kate jumped when she felt Thatcher touch her arm. She turned and looked up at him.

"Luigi told her their family was waiting for them. That they needed their mother," her voice cracked at the word mother, and something deep pinged within her.

She had never witnessed such raw emotion from a woman, had never seen what the bonds of motherhood could entail. Her own mother had been objective at best and impersonal at worst. There had been no love lost between them. It was more of an arrangement than a relationship. There were things expected of Kate, and there were things expected of her mother. But there was no love.

To see what such motherly love could do to such a strong woman as Rosa Salvatore had Kate's heart racing, wondering at the strength of such a love. Kate wondered if she would ever feel that way, if she would ever even have the opportunity to know a mother's love because she would have children of her own. She watched Thatcher as he watched Luigi comfort his wife, and the thought became more solid in her mind. Only weeks before, the thought would have been ludicrous. But now Katharine Cavanaugh had taken a lover where she had never thought it possible. She had found room in her life for him. What if she found room there for a family?

Would Thatcher marry her?

She had been thinking about it for several days now. Not seriously, of course. She didn't want to smother him with any questions about commitment and making her a respectable woman. They had been driven to an inevitable passion in a moment of deepest emotional turmoil. She wouldn't hold him to a standard that she did not hold herself to. If he wanted to marry her, she would accept him. She knew that now. If he did not wish to marry her, she would live with that. She wasn't sure she could bear it, but she would survive.

Perhaps theirs was only a passing love affair, an explosion of an attraction that could not be held back. She doubted it. Even as the thought formed in her mind, she shoved it aside as impossible. Thatcher did not seem like a man capable of such passing pleasures. She suspected that when he loved, he loved deeply. Just as he had carried a sixteen-year-old pain as fresh as if it had happened yesterday, Thatcher would not love lightly.

She tugged on his sleeve. "We should give them some time," she said and started in the direction of the door. She stopped at the well outside, dipping her hands and arms into the spillover bucket that sat there. She scrubbed off the flour and dough, feeling her skin crack as it dried out her skin. She shook her hands and dried them against her apron. Thatcher stood behind her when she finally straightened, his eyes squinting in the sun as he watched her.

"I was told the vessel will make port in Palermo by morning. You will need to go to the British naval quarters there and alert them to Murat's movements as soon as you land," he said.

"I will?" she asked, a grin coming to her lips. "Will you not accompany me to the naval barracks?"

Thatcher seemed to hesitate, but then his usual grin came to his face. She thought it wobbled for a moment, but then it could have just been the warmth of the noon sun getting to him. And he likely hadn't eaten for hours, and hunger had a way of upsetting a person. She could relate.

"I reckon the likes of an American in a British naval office is as wise an idea as drinking downstream from a cow pasture."

She laughed at his odd statement. "I reckon not," she said, attempting to match his flat accent.

He laughed at her now.

"How did you do it?" she asked, and his laughter died away. She regretted asking the question, but it burned at her. How had he done it? Surely he hadn't come up with the money to pay for passage. And if he had, where had he secured it? Was it stolen? She had heard tales of brazen American ways, but she didn't think thievery was among them. Especially not when it came to Thatcher.

She thought she saw him hesitate again, but then he smiled.

"You always need to gather information, don't you, Katharine Cavanaugh, great spy for the War Office?"

She liked the way he teased her, his casual grin and mischievous gaze doing more to her senses than any touch ever could.

"And you are always jesting, Matthew Thatcher," she said in return.

He waggled his eyebrows at her. "I reckon you're right," he said, shuffling his feet in the dirt. "It came to my attention that I had some valuable farming knowledge that I bartered in exchange for passage."

Kate raised an eyebrow at him. "Farming knowledge?"

Thatcher grinned and nodded. "It appears so," he said. He crossed his arms over his chest, nodding his head as if he were entirely sure of himself.

"What kind of knowledge?" she asked, taking a step towards him as she put her fisted hands on her hips, tilting her chin with just a measure of superiority.

Thatcher's smile faded. "It is not something to be

discussed with a lady," he said, turning away from her as if scandalized that she would ask.

She giggled at his game, pulling on his arm to get him to turn back to her. "Come now, Thatcher, what was it?"

He scoffed at her and brushed at her hands as if to shake her off like a piece of lint.

"I will not have my reputation ruined by your scandalous behavior, Lady Stirling," he said, his voice a pitch above its usual deep tones, his hands brushing harder at hers.

She laughed then , the sound full within her, and she tilted her head back to let it loose.

"You are a terrible sport, Mr. Thatcher," she said, when she had gained her breath.

He only smiled at her. "We'll see what you say later when I decide not to lick that small space at the back of your knee," he said, his voice suddenly dropping to a whisper.

Kate blushed instantly, the heat spreading across her face in a flash. It had been determined rather quickly that Kate did indeed enjoy it when Thatcher trailed his tongue along the sensitive skin at the backs of her knees, but to hear him talk of it out in broad daylight for anyone to hear, had her sensibilities pricked. But more, she didn't want him to refrain from the activity.

"You wouldn't dare!" she whispered back.

He smiled. "Are you sure?"

He turned away then , his strides long as he moved across the yard.

"Thatcher!" she screeched, picking up her skirts to chase after him.

CHAPTER 11

*T*hatcher found himself standing in the front yard of Luigi and Rosa's farm once again, the moon and stars taking their place in the night sky above him.

He hadn't had enough time. Deep inside him he knew he was doing the right thing. He knew that this was the only way he could save Kate before Murat's men moved into the north for battle. He just couldn't let happen to her what he had let happen to Thomas. But he hadn't had enough time.

He wanted more hours with her. He wanted more days with her. He wanted more anything with her. But here he was, standing once again in the front yard, waiting for Rosa and Luigi and Kate to emerge from the house, so they could begin their long trek into port on foot, avoiding any detection at all costs.

This was his last mission. This was the last thing he had to do. He had to get Kate to that ship safely. He had to see her on board. And then it didn't matter. That's what he kept telling himself. Once he completed this last mission, it wouldn't matter what happened to him, because the woman he loved would be gone. She would be somewhere safe, and he would have gotten her there. And that was all that mattered.

He tilted his head back, looking up into the inky blackness of the sky perforated with shimmering pinpoints of light. All of the stars were out tonight to see them safely on their way. The moon even hung nearly full in the sky, its rays a beckon on the road down to the port. It was all there to see them safely off. And he hated all of it. He hated that this needed to happen, and he hated that he was doing it. But then thoughts of Thomas flooded his mind, and he knew he wouldn't have done anything else. He loved Kate, and he needed to make sure she was safe.

They could risk staying. They could risk remaining in Naples. It was unlikely Murat's men would make it any farther south, but there was always the possibility. When they had set out to go fishing in the ravine that day, Thatcher knew some part of him understood the danger. His own father had warned him time and again not to go down in the ravine. He had told him it was dangerous. But he hadn't listened then , and Thomas had died.

Thatcher was listening now. Murat's men would be in the north, cutting off any chance of escape through the mountains, across France, and into Le Havre. The only way they had was by ship to Sicily and the British navy. But passage on a ship had cost a price, a precious price that Thatcher did not hesitate to give.

"What is it that has brought such a foul look to your face?"

Thatcher turned at the sound of Kate's voice, and like the night that he had waited for her in the front yard to accompany her on the mission to the masked gala, she stood in the doorway to the house, silhouetted by the light of the lamps beyond and the stars and moon above. Tonight she wore an altered gown of wool in black and gray tones, and her hair was tucked under the gray felt of one of Luigi's caps. She looked terrible, and yet, Thatcher had completely forgotten what she had asked for in that moment as he fell in love with her all over again.

"I beg your pardon?" he said, turning more fully to face her.

Kate smiled, her teeth white in the glow of the moon. "What are you thinking about? You look so glum."

She approached him, but he noticed how careful she was to keep a certain distance between them. He wanted to kiss her, just one more time before he had to let her go, but he just couldn't risk it. He just couldn't do it. If anyone should see, it may risk the entire mission. And he couldn't do that. He couldn't be so reckless when it came to Kate.

"Woolgathering, I suppose," he mumbled. "That's quite a fetching costume you have on there. You wouldn't fancy a dance would you?"

He tried a turn at his most regal British accent, but he feared it had come out garbled and morose. But it made Kate laugh, the sound like the strains of the softest music, and his heart lifted if only for a second before it came crashing down around him with the enormity of it all. That may be the last time he heard her laugh.

"Do you reckon we have time?" she asked, mimicking his own accent. She was far better at it than he, her acting abilities having been honed for years doing work for the War Office.

"There's always enough time for one more dance," he said.

It was foolish. It was foolish and reckless and irrational. He shouldn't do this. But a part of him just wanted to feel her, just wanted to touch her one more time. He bowed before her and, rising, extended a hand in her direction.

"May I have this dance, my lady?" he said.

Kate smiled, curtsied, and placed her hand into his. She stepped into his arms as if she had always done it, as if it were perfectly natural to dance with him in the moonlight with the only music the sound of the wind blowing in off the port, rustling the leaves of the stunted olive trees in the grove beyond them. Kate continued to smile as he shuffled into a kind of waltz. Their footsteps were not precise, but as neither of them was truly paying attention to their feet, it seemed to work. He watched her face, watched the happiness that glowed there. It sent a pang directly to his heart, knowing that in a matter of hours, he would deceive her. Had already deceived her. And soon she would know. And it would kill him. It would slice him through in the worst way possible.

But then Kate would be safe. Then Kate would be on a ship and on her way to people who could protect her until she returned to England. That was all that mattered. He just needed to keep repeating it.

He spun her about once more and stopped at the sound of clapping coming from the direction of the house. His abrupt halt had Kate tipping into him, her body coming against him in a way propriety would not allow but in which he found immense pleasure. He absorbed the feel of her, took in the scent of her, memorized the way her smile lifted the corners of her wide mouth. She stepped back, and even in the moonlight, he saw her blush as she turned to Luigi and Rosa who still clapped for them in the doorway of the farmhouse.

Thatcher turned to look and saw Luigi and Rosa standing between two cases packed for travel. Both wore shades of black and gray, and Rosa's hair was carefully covered in a black kerchief. Rosa's tears of the day before were long past as she realized she would soon see her sons again. She would soon hold them in her arms. Now, she was a woman ready for the stealthy journey down the hillside and to the waiting ship that would take them to Sicily and her family.

And it was with this realization that Thatcher most

wished he was traveling with them. When he most wished he could see the look on Rosa Salvatore's face when she was reunited with her babies, as she called them, after such a long separation.

As if she sensed he was thinking about her, Rosa walked over to him, grabbed at his neck, and pulled him down to her level, much as she'd done the first day they'd arrived. She gripped his chin in her hand, and in a most serious tone, spoke of something he could not understand. He looked over the top of her head at Kate for explanation, but when his eyes met hers, she brought a hand to her mouth and turned abruptly away. Puzzled, he looked to Luigi.

"She says you will make a good husband to Lady Katharine, and you will make fine babies," Luigi said.

Rosa patted him once on the cheek and released him. Thatcher straightened with a shuffle of his feet, watching Kate's back as she continued to look away from them. Rosa's words had driven the last splinter through his heart, leaving it wounded and vulnerable. He could only imagine what Kate felt just then , thinking that soon they would be free and Rosa's words could ring true.

He needed to see her face at the same time he couldn't bear to see her face. He stepped toward her, but she was already turning about, a smile across her face. It wobbled slightly, but the force of it was unquestionable.

"That's lovely, Rosa, but I fear if we had children they would be very tall," she said this in English while she looked at him, but then she turned to Rosa and presumably repeated it in Italian.

Rosa let out a bark of laughter before putting one hand on her hip, the other shaking a finger at Thatcher. Kate smiled harder.

"She says it doesn't matter how tall they get, they're still babies to their parents," Kate relayed to him, finally turning to look at him fully.

He hadn't thought he could love her any more than he already did, but just then , she proved him wrong.

"And those babies will not wait for us forever. Let's go, comrades," Luigi said, shaking a triumphant fist into the air.

Thatcher looked at the squat farmhouse that had been their sanctuary for the past few weeks. The lamps had been extinguished, and Luigi moved to shut the door carefully as if he expected to return in just a few hours. Luigi turned and caught Thatcher watching him. He smiled.

"Alberto and his son will take care of the farm for us. Perhaps one day we will be back. And if not, I think Alberto would make an excellent farmer of olives. What think you?"

Luigi laughed and picked up their traveling cases, offering his elbow to Rosa. The pair sauntered down the yard and into the passage that would lead them to the port. He walked over to Kate, offering her his own elbow.

"Shall we?" he said, his heart breaking as she slipped her hand through his arm.

"We shall," she said, and they began their last walk together down the hill.

THE TRIP down the hillside was markedly uneventful. Kate didn't know if the inhabitants of the hills around Naples were simply worn out from the festival for San Gennaro or if they just preferred to retire early, but the pass down the hill had been silent and empty. The light of the moon lit the road as if it were daylight, and Rosa and Luigi plodded ahead of them with certainty.

When the fields of olive trees and outbuildings faded into the congestion of the port, Thatcher took lead, striding ahead of Luigi and Rosa, while she remained behind, watching their rear position. The night was unusually quiet, and for a moment, Kate didn't believe it could be that easy. She expected at least someone to be out that night. The hour was not unbearably late, and from what little she had seen and heard of the port town, life was lively after the sun had set. The quiet was eerie and unnerving, and she kept her senses fully alert, not allowing her mind to be distracted by the sight of Thatcher's rear position in his tight fitting breeches.

Thatcher slowed as they entered the port proper, moving with calculated even steps, reducing the sound produced by the impact of his boots on the cobblestones. Luigi and Rosa mimicked him although they wore boots with soles softened from years of hard work, and the impact against the stone was not as great. Kate moved carefully behind them, watching Thatcher as she scanned the houses and buildings behind them.

She could smell the sea now, hear the water lapping in the distance against the great wooden piers of the port. She looked up to check the position of the moon, and that was when she heard it.

Her gaze moved to Thatcher to see if he had heard it, too. He had stopped at the corner of a large stucco building, his body rigid in the moonlight.

There were footsteps, loud, clear, and ringing footsteps only feet from their position. The footsteps carried an authority that required no visual to understand. Kate laid a hand on the shoulders of Rosa and Luigi, stilling them with her touch. The older people froze, their eyes riveted on Thatcher. Kate saw out of the corner of her eye as Luigi took Rosa's hand into his. Kate's heart constricted at the sight, but she pushed the thought away, moving silent around the couple to gain better perspective from Thatcher's position.

She drew close to his shoulder, not daring to move her head any further around him to see who it was that might be coming. But then the footsteps were joined by other footsteps, just as loud but not quite carrying the same tone of authority. And then suddenly there was a burst of laughter. The sound startled her so much, she bumped into Thatcher. His arm came out to steady her, and in that moment, she took the opportunity to peer around the edge of the building.

The soft glow of lamplight fell onto the cobblestones from what appeared to be a pub of some sort on what Kate could only decide must be the city center, a large open space of bricked walkway with a fountain taking up residence in the center. The area was outlined with the facades of various shops and pubs and the odd residence. And stumbling from one such establishment was a group of men in uniforms. The moonlight did not penetrate far enough into the square for her to get a clear idea of who the gentlemen may be, but the sense of uniforms was unquestionable.

She pulled her head back, looking up at Thatcher. She knew by the look on his face that he had seen the uniforms as well. She tilted her head, eyes questioning, hoping he understood her meaning.

What were they going to do?

They had to cross the square in order to reach the wharf and the waiting ship that would carry them to safety. They could try to go around the square, but taking such a circuitous route increased the probability that they would be seen, or worse, caught. They must go through the square, she was certain of it.

The sound of laughter ricocheted through the empty square once more, and she darted her head around Thatcher's shoulder to get another visual. And that's when she realized two things. She drew her head back and looked at Thatcher. His eyes burned with the same understanding.

The first important thing of note, the one that at that moment gave her the greatest hope, was the glint of moonlight on water that could just be seen between the buildings on the opposite side of the square. The water was close. They had only to cross the square.

But the second important thing of note largely ruled out the hopeful qualities of the first.

One of the uniformed men was the man who had questioned them upon their arrival and who was affectionately known as 'the general' by Luigi and Rosa. He was unmistakable as he shuffled about with his cronies in the moonlit square.

Kate felt a tapping at her shoulder and turned, bending to reach Rosa's upturned face.

"It's the general," she whispered. "I can hear him. He must have been frequenting Madame Louisa's." She finished her sentence with a grave nod of her head as Luigi crossed himself.

Kate determined Madame Louisa's was an establishment of ill repute and turned back to Thatcher. He looked at her, and she leaned up on her tiptoes to whisper Rosa's message.

Thatcher looked at her and mimed drinking. She shrugged. She didn't know if the establishment offered such pleasantries as drink or if the men had imbibed. Thatcher turned back in the direction of their obstacle and waited. When the next burst of laughter came out, they both ducked their heads about the corner and watched.

One man was on all fours, his jacket pulled up over his head so it covered his ears, while another man straddled his back and pretended to slap his bottom. The man on all fours whinnied and hawed as if he were a donkey. They ducked back, sharing a knowing look.

The men had, indeed, imbibed.

Kate stood on tiptoe once more to press her lips to Thatcher's ear.

"Unbutton my gown," she said, indicating the row of buttons that traveled down the back of her dress. She turned slightly, so he could reach them. When nothing happened, she cast a glance over her shoulder to see Thatcher's eyes had grown wide. She frowned at him but leaned forward to explain.

"I'll get their attention and draw them over here. When they round the corner, we'll immobilize them."

Thatcher raised an eyebrow and indicated the number four with his fingers. She frowned again.

"Yes, there are four of them, but there are two of us. We'll each take two. It will work," she whispered feverishly.

Thatcher shook his head, but he spun her around and loosened the buttons at the top of her gown. The bodice slipped, leaving one shoulder bare and her bosom adequately exposed. She looked down at herself to find her chemise poking out from underneath the dress. Pulling her felt hat down to disguise her features better, she gave Thatcher a wink as she went around the corner of the building.

She was careful to falter a little, leaning on the building for support. She wanted to look weak and helpless and, more importantly, smaller. She knew the moment she was spotted as the whining donkey man stopped his song mid-heehaw. The square fell silent except for the sounds of her own awkward steps against the cobblestone and the sporadic shuffle of a booted foot. For good measure, she held a hand to her forehead, looking up through her lashes as she let her face melt into a sinful pout with just the slightest hint of despair. She wasn't sure how much of her face was visible in the shadows, but she knew a man's mind never lacked for imagination.

The donkey man and his rider stared at her while the

fourth uniformed man and the general leaned in thorough casualness against the front of what Kate assumed was Madame Louisa's with its discreetly shuttered windows and closed doors. The lamplight from the taverns on either side of Madame Louisa's provided enough illumination under the eaves of the building for Kate to make out the features of the general's face and ascertain that she had, in fact, gotten his attention. Her heart thumped with the realization, but her pulse remained steady. She was a seasoned professional, and this was a thoroughly calculated and well thought-out mission.

She stumbled, coming down on one knee, while she let out a soft mewling sound. She had never made such a sound in her life, but it made her sound pitifully mournful. She gained her feet and slowly, painfully, achingly slowly, bent and lifted the hem of her dress as if inspecting her stockings for a tear. She drew the material up her leg, moving with the speed of a decrepit dowager in a crowded ballroom. The hem reached her knee, and she held it there for a moment, turning her foot from side to side. She knew the light from the moon and the neighboring taverns illuminated her enough to be seen but not with any great detail. So she dropped the hem of her skirt and let her head drop back, a giggly laugh escaping her lips. She swept a hand dramatically to her loosened neckline, fingered the lace of her chemise.

"I'm not wearing stockings," she said, loud enough so the men across the square could hear.

She thought the donkey man and his rider would fall over at any moment, but then a muffled sound came from behind her that sounded awfully much like Thatcher cursing. There was no way the men on the other side of the square could hear, but she had heard it clearly enough. Luigi must have translated what she had said. A smile came to her lips at the thought, and she looked back at the uniformed men.

The general had straightened, and adjusting his jacket, he motioned to the other three men. There was no protest or signs of defiance as the rider helped up the donkey man and, with the third uniformed man, pushed through the door of Madame Louisa's.

Kate's heart raced now as she stood alone in the square. The odds had suddenly improved greatly and in their favor. She smiled as she turned, hiding her head coquettishly behind her bared shoulder. She started to walk away, slowly, very, very, very slowly. Her pulse now fluttered in her ears, and she was sure it was loud enough to be heard across the square. But as she made the slow walk back to the corner of the building, the sound of the general's footfalls were distinctly definitive above the sound of her heartbeat. She turned the corner, and as soon as the shadows swallowed her, she righted her dress. She reached behind her, but fingers were already there straightening the garment. Kate cast a smile of thanks at Rosa, who only nodded with a sly wink.

The general's footsteps had quickened, becoming louder with each step. Kate tugged on Thatcher's shoulder, holding up a single finger and puffing out her chest while casting an expression of superiority on her face. Thatcher's own expression went from confusion to understanding and then a satisfied grin. And before the general could clear the corner of the building, Thatcher's fist brought the man to his knees. Kate heard someone gasp and thought it may have been her, but when Thatcher aimed a kick at the general's head, all sound froze in her throat. She backed up, finding Luigi to one side of her and Rosa on the other, each with a hand on one of her arms. The three of them stood there and stared as Thatcher took the general down until he lay unconscious on the cobblestones. He finally turned, and Kate felt her eyes widen on him. He only shrugged.

"You shouldn't have told him you weren't wearing stockings," he whispered. "Let's go."

Kate shook herself loose, pulling Luigi and Rosa in front of her. Luigi grabbed the case he had set down to take Kate's arm and once more urged Rosa forward as Thatcher walked quickly into the square. The water was close, and soon Kate heard the unmistakable sounds of an active wharf. On the other side of the square, the streets grew thick with pubs and taverns, their doors open wide to the water as sailors and seamen and traders and the like spilled from one establishment to the other. Kate caught sight of a streetwalker or two entertaining gentlemen along the wharf, and she urged Rosa and Luigi on, their feet eating up the cobblestones as they gained the pier.

Thatcher seemed to know where he was going as he traveled the length of a dock and turned down another. She followed, her feet sure across the wooden planks. The pier was littered with carefully coiled ropes and nets and stacked wooden crates. The odd sailor was discovered lounging behind some of the crates or in the unique case, sleeping on coiled rope. Kate thought that an odd sleeping space but figured his other options may be equally as comfortable.

Thatcher paused for a moment behind one wooden crate almost as tall as he was at the end of the dock. She looked around but did not see anything. She looked behind them and still saw nothing. She reached over Luigi's and Rosa's heads to tap him on the shoulder. When he turned to look at her, he raised a finger telling her to wait.

She frowned but did as she was told. Their position was somewhat vulnerable, and she looked about her for a possible weapon or a place to hide. They were at the end of one of the docks. No ship was tied to the pier, but the dock did contain an unusually large amount of waiting cargo. It suddenly occurred to her that they may have beaten the ship to the dock. She looked out over the water just as a small vessel moved into view from the edges of the port. Kate didn't know much about ships, but this one did not appear to be overly large. She wasn't sure what sort of ship was needed for the journey to Sicily, but she supposed it must not be a very grand one. The island could not be more than a day's journey by sea, and in the sheltered curve of the mainland, the journey could not be as fraught with danger as an ocean voyage.

The ship grew larger as it approached the dock, its sails gleaming white and regal in the moonlight. She had been studying the ship so hard, she had not noticed the dockhands that soon flooded the dock they stood on. She crowded closer to Rosa and Luigi as ropes suddenly flew through the air, narrowly missing her head. Amidst shouts of directions, the ship pulled into the dock with a smoothness that belied the skill of its captain. The gangplank struck the dock with a charge just in front of them, and once more, Kate jumped, startled by the magnificent sound.

Thatcher, who had watched the entire scene from his perch behind the wooden crate, finally turned about. He smiled at Luigi and Rosa.

"It's time to board," he said. "Your family is waiting."

Rosa and Luigi did not hesitate. Rosa latched a hand onto Luigi's shoulder and all but pulled him in the direction of the ship. Thatcher smiled as he watched them go, and then he turned to her. She thought she saw a moment of hesitation about him, an air of sadness, but then he smiled, brightly and hugely, just as he always did.

Sweeping a hand in front of him, he said, "Ladies first."

She returned his smile and carefully moved through the dockhands that carried cargo up the gangplank. As she passed Thatcher though, he suddenly reached out and grabbed her. Once more she got the odd sense of hesitation from him, but then he kissed her, his mouth warm and sure on hers, and she sank into him, absorbing the kiss that was now so familiar to her.

He released her as suddenly as he had grabbed her, and she stumbled back into the rush of dockhands. She made her way up the gangplank to see Luigi and Rosa on the main deck speaking to a young man, who was indicating grandly the features of the ship, as if it were such a great treat to have guests on board their merchant vessel.

It wasn't until the gangplank had been raised that Kate realized Thatcher was not behind her.

CHAPTER 12

*K*ate rushed to the side of the ship, her hands gripping the railing as she peered over the edge. The ship had already pushed out, the dock some distance away. She saw Thatcher immediately. He stood a head taller than any of the dockhands that still swarmed the pier. He had removed his hat, and the moonlight shone on his golden hair. And he watched her, a look of sheer emptiness on his features.

Something in her ceased. She wanted to scream. She wanted to rail. She wanted to do something. But suddenly, she couldn't move. She couldn't think. She couldn't do anything. The dock was slipping farther and farther away. Her fingers dug into the wood of the ship, but she did not notice the splinters piercing her skin. She saw only Thatcher, growing smaller as the ship moved out to sea.

What was he doing? Why wasn't he on board with them?

And then she became aware of another person on the dock with Thatcher, a painfully thin man of short stature. He stood just behind Thatcher, but he shifted suddenly, his features coming into the light.

Scevola.

The breath froze in her lungs, her stomach heaving.

What had Thatcher done?

Suddenly her mind raced. What had she missed? What had she overlooked? Thatcher had said he had bartered information, agricultural information, for their passage on this merchant vessel to Sicily. She had accepted it as she had not believed that Thatcher could lie to her, but now, everything seemed wrong. What agrarian information was valuable enough to provide passage to four people on a ship? Passage that may cause the owner of the ship to fall under serious reprimands?

And then , barely discernible at the distance the ship had now reached from the dock, Kate saw Scevola place a hand on Thatcher's shoulder, and everything came crashing down around her. The conversation Thatcher had had with Scevola that night at the masked gala, the rumors of Scevola's relations with men, and Thatcher's mysterious disappearance the previous morning.

He had gone to make a deal with Scevola to get passage for Kate and the Salvatores to Sicily. And in that deal, he had sacrificed himself.

And then Kate did scream. She screamed for all of bloody Italy and Murat himself to hear.

"Thatcher, I love you!" she screamed, her words piercing the black of night like the wail of a mythical siren.

* * *

ALTHOUGH THE SHIP had moved out into the port, Thatcher heard Kate's cry as if she were standing next to him. It landed with physical pain, lancing his heart with the deadly precision of a lethal blow. Scevola's hand was a hateful weight on his shoulder. He stood there, unmoving, the taste of Kate's last kiss fading on his lips.

And he hated himself.

He hated himself for falling in love with her. He hated himself for not telling her. And he hated himself for finally, after all these years, protecting the person he loved. Kate was safe now. The ship would take her to Sicily and the British navy. He had finally done the right thing. A piece of him lifted, the weight of Thomas' death no longer bearing down on him.

Only now, a new weight pressed against him, and he struggled against it. He would never see her again. He would never feel the smoothness of her skin, never hear the sound of her laugh, never watch her face as it lit with a smile.

He only hoped that one day, she would finally discover what it was she wanted, and then she would forget him. She would be happy and safe. That was all that mattered.

"The ship will arrive in Palermo by morning," Scevola said from beside him, and Thatcher felt the bile rise in his throat. "We must leave now. I cannot be seen on this dock."

Scevola turned away, and Thatcher thought it to be as simple as that. But then Scevola paused and turned back, extending that one finger with the too long nail to trail it down the shoulder of his jacket.

"I shall let you get settled tonight, American, but tomorrow night, I expect payment for services rendered."

Thatcher made no indication that he had heard the other man, moving his gaze towards the horizon and the disappearing ship racing to meet it.

* * *

THE HOURS PASSED, but Kate did not notice. She sat on the

deck of the ship, the hard wooden planks unforgiving against her backside. The wind whipped at her hair, her felt hat long gone, and tore at her dress, but she did not notice or care. She sat, staring at the spot of railing where she had stood as she had watched the distance between her and the man she loved grow wider and wider. Sailors prowled the deck, moving about her with unnoticed grace. She heard the calls from the men up in the lines and the hails from the captain at the helm. But she only saw Thatcher standing on the dock, Scevola at his side.

"I did not want to marry Luigi. Did I tell you this?"

Kate looked up, her eyes not comprehending what she saw. Rosa stood above her. Her familiar round shape distinct against the backdrop of the starry night sky. She opened her mouth to speak, but nothing came out. Rosa smiled and carefully set her body down on the deck beside Kate, her short legs poking out from the folds of her skirt. She sat with her hands folded in her lap, her back against the wall next to Kate's, her hands softly folded in her lap as if she held conversations on the deck of merchant vessels every day.

"I wanted to marry Eustachio Basilio Cantu. A fantastic name, no?"

Kate continued to stare at her, this woman who for weeks had drilled instructions into her head in a language Kate had only learned a few years before. And now the woman sat beside her as if they usually had casual chats on the decks of ships. For a moment, Kate was distracted from the incessant ache in her chest.

"Fantastic," Kate finally murmured.

"He was a butcher's son. You know what this means? I could have lived in town!" She said the word for town with a dramatic flair of her arm rising into the air. She smiled at Kate. "But I did not marry Eustachio. You know why."

Kate did not hear the natural inflection in Rosa's voice at that last part, and she thought it was not a question.

"I beg your pardon?" Kate said, when Rosa did not continue.

"You know why I did not marry Eustachio. You feel it now."

Kate only blinked at her. She felt what now? She felt dead inside. Hollow. Like someone had split her open and scooped out her innards like some kind of squash.

"I feel awful," she said to Rosa.

Rosa nodded. "And what else?"

Kate looked about them on the ship, noticing for the first time the captain at the helm above them on the quarterdeck. Seeing him standing there made her realize there must be others on board the ship, others who knew that three refugees were being smuggled to Sicily. She suddenly took in the enormity of it, of everything that Thatcher had arranged to get them from Naples to Sicily. It wasn't as if they had simply boarded a vessel for a pleasure jaunt through the Mediterranean. This was a working merchant vessel, and their very presence put the livelihood of these men at stake. And Thatcher had somehow negotiated it all.

And for the briefest of moments, she smiled. Thatcher was a remarkable spy.

Kate realized she had not answered Rosa when the woman poked her in the ribs with an elbow. She rubbed at her side as if offended, but right then , she couldn't muster up the energy to feel anything besides the yawning emptiness swallowing her.

"Nothing," she said to Rosa, suddenly angry that this short little woman would prod her so.

"You're lying. You may not know you are lying, but you are."

Kate looked at her sharply. "That's rather bold," she said

and stopped herself. "And what gives you the right to tell me what I'm feeling?" She pointed a finger at Rosa and moved it about in a circle as if indicating the entire situation before them.

Rosa only blinked at her. "I tell you how you feel because you do not know it yourself."

Kate straightened her shoulders against the wood at her back. "I know exactly how I feel. I am Katharine Cavanaugh, Captain Hadley's daughter, and I am an agent for the British War Office. That's how I feel."

Rosa shook her head. "That is what you are. Not how you feel. You do not know the difference."

Kate felt properly chastised, and as she did not feel like feeling anything other than the cold hand of endless agony that smothered her, she turned away, looking once more at the spot of railing where she had last seen Thatcher.

"What is it? What is it you are feeling right there?" Rosa pointed at the bit of railing on which Kate focused. "You even say it right there."

Kate only frowned at her, and Rosa mumbled something that may have been translated as blasted woman.

"My mother, she say to me, Rosa, marry a man with a skill. You live in a pretty house in town and never have to work in dirt. She say this to me. And me, I say Mama, I do this thing you tell me to do. Because I want to make you happy. So I say I want to marry Eustachio, the butcher's son. I say I do not want to marry Luigi. But this is a lie, you see."

Kate said, "Your mother wanted you to marry the butcher's son?"

Rosa nodded. "Oh yes, and I agree with her, because what she say make sense. But I forget something."

Kate was now fully engrossed with what Rosa was saying, a long forgotten conversation with Thatcher bubbling to the surface.

"What did you forget?" Kate asked.

"I forget to ask myself what I wanted. It does no good if it makes sense, because if I do not want it, I will be unhappy. Only worse, I will not know why I am unhappy, because I have done everything I had been told."

Kate felt her mouth hanging open, but she did not care. "And then what happened?" she whispered, not knowing why she was whispering, but she daren't move her eyes from Rosa as if at any moment the woman may say something of extreme value.

"I marry Luigi," Rosa said.

Kate blinked, moving her head back as if she had been slapped. "But what happened in the middle? Why did you marry Luigi when your mother told you to marry Eustachio?"

Rosa shrugged. "I just ask myself what I wanted. And I wanted Luigi."

"But why?" Kate's voice was perilously close to imploring, but she did not care. She knew this woman held the secret to something that Kate did not understand, and she needed answers. "Why did you marry Luigi?"

"For the same reason you will do something terribly brave when we reach Sicily," Rosa said.

Kate shook her head. "What?"

"What did you just tell the whole world?" Rosa said, gesturing toward the railing.

Kate looked at the structure as if it could give her an answer. And then it did. "I love him," she whispered, thinking of her hysterical cry as they pulled out of port.

Rosa slapped a hand to her thigh. "That is why I marry Luigi. I love him. And he had a cute, what is it you say in English? I believe you call it a bottom. He have a very nice bottom when he was a young man. Oh! Eustachio have not so nice bottom. I choose Luigi."

Kate had stopped listening. She loved Thatcher. She wanted Thatcher. It was perfectly clear to her with the suddenness of an afternoon storm in summer. She wanted Thatcher. She wanted to marry Thatcher and have children with him and raise them with him and take over Cook's kitchen so she could make pasta like Rosa had shown her. She didn't know where that last part had come from, but she liked how it fit with the rest of what she wanted.

And more than that, she wanted Thatcher with her, beside her, on every mission she undertook for the War Office. Thatcher wasn't the husband she had always thought she didn't have room for. Thatcher was the partner she had always needed. The one who would stand beside her on every mission she would undertake for the War Office for the rest of her life.

"Rosa," Kate said as the pinks of dawn began to light the sky around them.

"Sì?" Rosa said.

"I'm going to do something very brave when we get to Sicily."

Rosa nodded, a knowing smile tugging at her lips. "And why is that?"

Kate looked toward the approaching dawn. "Because I finally figured out what Katharine Cavanaugh wants."

CHAPTER 13

*T*he gangway had barely settled on the dock in Palermo when Kate's feet struck the wooden planks of the pier. She hiked her skirts far higher than propriety deemed acceptable, but she was in a hurry. Propriety be damned.

She swerved between bustling dockhands and working seamen. She heard the clip clop of Rosa and Luigi as they scurried behind her. The morning had dawned with the clarity of a typical Mediterranean day, the breeze salty and fresh, the skies dotted with translucent clouds. But the angelic atmosphere was lost on Kate as she moved through the throng swarming the wharf, approaching the dock master's station.

The dock master was a tall man with gangly arms and overly large elbows that stuck out from his sides in earnest, making him appear to have clubs as arms. He was well dressed if a bit rumpled from the already growing humidity, and he was deep in conversation with another gentleman of average height and appearance. When the dock master did not indicate he had seen her at her approach, she took the only measure left to her.

She slammed her fist onto the dock master's station.

The gangly man and the average man both jumped to Kate's satisfaction, turning round eyes on her.

"Good morning, gentlemen," Kate said in English, her accent crisp, her enunciation perfect.

The two men looked behind her at the merchant vessel that had just docked and back at her.

"I beg your pardon, miss," said the dock master, clearly confused as to how passengers had disembarked from a merchant vessel.

"It's lady actually," she said, "I have need to speak with the British commodore. I will wait for you to arrange transport to his residence."

The dock master did not move, and Kate felt Rosa's stare on her. She turned her head to look at the older woman to find her smiling broadly while Luigi looked on confused, their two traveling cases tucked under his arms.

Kate turned back to the dock master as Luigi murmured, "What is she doing?" to which Rosa responded, "She is doing something brave. Now hush!"

The dock master continued to stare as Kate blinked expectantly.

"Do we have a problem, sir?" she said finally.

And the dock master shook himself as if to come out of a fog. "I'm terribly sorry. You said you wish to see the British commodore?"

"Yes, it's a matter of state business," she said.

The dock master absently waved a hand at the average man he had been speaking to, sending the man off in a dash toward the street and the line of cabs waiting there. In the same motion, he snapped his fingers at a boy squatting on a wooden crate at his feet. The boy was covered in filth, and as soon as he stood, his odor reached Kate's nostrils. The lad must have been no more than eight or nine years old, and his clothes were mere rags hanging on his gaunt frame. Something inside Kate clenched at the sight of him.

"I'll send a message ahead to let the commodore know you are coming. Whom shall I say is calling?"

Kate looked at the small boy. "Ka--" she hesitated, her newfound resolve warring with a long hardened expectation that until now had pushed on her relentlessly. The little boy continued to look at her, and she remembered what Rosa had said about her and Thatcher making beautiful babies.

Kate looked at the dock master. "Tell him Captain Hadley's daughter, Katharine, wishes to speak with him." And then she turned to the boy. "And tell the commodore Captain Hadley's daughter expects him to tip you well."

The boy's eyes lit with excitement before he turned and disappeared into the crowds.

* * *

THE COMMODORE'S barracks were more opulent than Kate would have assumed, but as the commander of the British fleet in the Mediterranean, she supposed his accommodations would reflect his position. His quarters were near enough to the wharf, in a two-story building of yellow stucco and slate tile roof with open windows in the front and a small portico, giving it more grandeur than the building seemed to want.

As the cab pulled up in front, a uniformed man in the familiar colors of the British navy emerged, sweeping down the steps to open the carriage door. However, as impatient as she was, Kate stepped down from the carriage even before the man had reached her. He stopped in front of her, tilting his head back, way back, to peer up at her.

"Captain Hadley's daughter?" he said, his voice as squeezed as his eyes were wide.

He was a short man with nondescript features smothered in bristly facial hair as if to make up for his lack of noteworthy attributes.

Kate nodded. "Please assist my companions," she said and left the man, whoever he was, blithering like an idiot at the open cab door.

Kate strode up the few steps leading into the front hall of the residence, noting its marble floors and polished wooden elements. Looking up, she spotted the commodore descending the steps, his hands brushing at the fabric of his jacket as if she had caught him as he finished dressing.

"Commodore," she said, her voice firm as it rang through the empty front hall.

The man faltered on the stairs and for a moment, she feared he would fall to his demise until he righted himself against the banister. The commodore was younger than she had expected and, more to her surprise, rather handsome. When he straightened, she noted his height, perhaps a couple of inches above her own, with wide shoulders and a trim waist, uncommon for a gentleman of his rank. Most commodores she had met had let themselves go soft about the middle as an increase in rank often meant a decrease in the need for physical activity. His thick brown hair was cut short and swept back from his face. He had a rather square forehead and a long nose, and Kate thought he must often be mistaken for appearing serious or worse, melancholy, when in fact it was just how his face was.

He appeared to be freshly shaven as in he had only shaved mere moments before Kate had stepped in the door. She looked about her for a clock, but she was fairly certain it was well into mid-morning, and the commodore should have been about by then .

"Countess," the commodore said, stepping off the last stair and bowing before her. "I apologize for my unkempt state," he continued, tucking his bicorn under his arm. "Things work a bit differently here in the Mediterranean, and it's not every day a countess, especially a countess who is the daughter of such an esteemed captain, appears on our doorstep."

Now that he was closer, she could see that his eyes were a deep brown and crinkled at the corners when he smiled, which he did now, although the smile looked forced and rather weak. But he was making an effort to accommodate her intrusion, so she returned his smile with one of her own.

"Thank you, Commodore, for receiving me. I have need of one of your ships," she said without preamble.

There was a commotion behind them as Rosa and Luigi made their way through the door, the clerk who had run out to greet them arguing with Luigi to assist with the traveling cases. When the argument spilled into the front hall, the clerk abruptly shut his mouth at the sight of the commodore. The clerk seemed to stare for a while, and Kate wondered if it were just an annoying habit of the clerk or if the commodore really had only dressed for her arrival, and the clerk was not used to seeing him in full uniform. Kate scanned the gold brocade and blue frock of the commodore's uniform jacket and did not note anything exceptional about it. Luigi took the clerk's moment of surprise to wrest the traveling cases out of his hands.

"Commodore, allow me to introduce my traveling companions, Rosa and Luigi Salvatore." She indicated the Salvatores, who nodded with smiles to the commodore.

"Good morning, Mr. and Mrs. Salvatore, welcome to Palermo," the commodore said. "Mayhew, please see that proper refreshments are brought to my office."

Mayhew seemed to squirm. "But, sir, we already brought a cart for--"

The commodore cut him off saying, "We'll have need of another. Quickly, man."

Mayhew took off toward the back of the building to where Kate assumed there were stairs leading to the kitchens below if that was how homes were structured here in Palermo. She honestly had no idea and didn't really care right then .

"You have need of a ship?" the commodore said, and Kate turned back to him.

He focused on her rather intently and, for the first time in hours, Kate felt like she would have honest help on the madcap idea she had brewed up in the long hours of their journey to Sicily.

"Yes, Commodore--" she stopped. "Oh dear, how impolite of me. I didn't even allow you to give me your name."

She gestured for him to relay his name.

"It's John Lynwood, my lady," he said with a nod.

"Splendid. Commodore Lynwood--" she stopped midsentence again, wondering for a moment if she were to be plagued with false starts around this man. "As in the Lynwoods of Heresford?"

The commodore seemed to hesitate, and he drew a large breath before nodding. "Yes, my lady, my father is the Earl of Heresford."

Kate leaned in, squinting her eyes as if to see better, while the commodore leaned back, away from her careful study.

"Jack?" she whispered, her eyes growing round the more she studied him.

The commodore swallowed and licked his lips uncomfortably. "For a moment, I thought you wouldn't notice," he said.

Kate straightened, a feeling of weightlessness overcoming

her in a flurry as emotions of varying size and color swept through her in a torrent, and she did the only thing she could think to do. She threw herself at the man. The commodore caught her neatly, awkwardly returning her embrace.

"Jack Lynwood!" she cried, and then she found she was actually crying, wrinkling and wetting the front of his dress uniform. "Oh God, Jack Lynwood, it's terrible. I love him, and he made a deal with a horrible man, and he sacrificed himself, and he didn't even ask me!" She stopped when she realized she wasn't really making sense. And more-- "How did you end up here?" she asked, looking about her as if she could see the entirety of the Mediterranean about them, "The last time I saw you, you were chasing Miranda with a frog, telling her to kiss it."

The commodore smiled that hesitant smile that didn't quite reach his eyes again. "I would have chased you and told you to kiss it, but I was rather afraid of you," he said, looking anywhere but at her.

Kate smiled, feeling her tears dry on her cheeks. "Little Jack Lynwood, all grown up. But you're a commodore! How did you manage that?"

His face went blank then , and his mouth moved into a grimace. "I really do not know," he said, his voice unusually quiet. "But what about you? You're a spy for the War Office just like your mother always said you would be. And now you need one of my ships. And I presume this gentleman you speak of is one Mr. Matthew Thatcher. An American actually."

Kate blinked. "How do you know his name?"

Instead of answering her, he looked behind her to where the Salvatores had been standing quietly. Kate had nearly forgotten about them.

Momentarily distracted, she said, "And perhaps some

food is in order. We haven't eaten since yesterday." She smiled sheepishly.

Jack gestured toward the hallway as he began to walk. Kate followed, looking behind her to ensure the Salvatores followed her.

"Your appearance is not entirely unexpected," Jack said in front of her, and Kate looked up at him.

"What do you mean?" she asked, her brow wrinkling.

Jack paused in front of a set of double doors before opening them to indicate they should enter. Kate walked in and stopped. Standing in front a bank of windows along the far wall stood a man that looked by all accounts like a beggar. She stopped, taking a step back, and looked to Jack for explanation. Jack was showing Rosa and Luigi to a sofa in front of the dormant fireplace in the room that appeared to be the commodore's office. It was tastefully decorated, if sparse of the more extraneous comforts of a house that made it seem lived in. A large desk sat opposite the fireplace and the seating arrangement, its surface lost amongst the sea of papers scattered across it. The beggar at the far window turned, and Kate almost shuddered at the appearance.

His clothes were torn and patched, his skin blackened with filth, and his hat would rival those of the haughtiest matrons in all of London society, with a great plume projecting from the top of it. And by Christ, he had a wooden leg.

"Commodore?" Kate said.

"Kate, allow me to introduce you to Captain Reginald Davis," Jack said, before leaning a hip against his desk and folding his arms casually across his chest.

Kate looked at the man with renewed inspection. "Captain?" she asked.

"Yes, and it's a pleasure to see you, Countess Stirling, although I had hoped to find you with that bloke, Thatcher, but I guess one out of two isn't terrible." His tone was surprisingly cultured and did not fit at all with the rest of his appearance. "Whereabouts would we find Mr. Thatcher?"

Kate blinked at the man. "Naples," she said, "But who are you?"

Davis smiled softly. "Once it was ascertained which ship it was that you and Mr. Thatcher boarded in Dover, the Duke of Lofton sent me after you," he said, referring to the father of her former partner, Alec Black, the Earl of Stryden. "It would do no good to lose two of our finest agents to the enemy,"

"Thatcher is not an agent for the War Office," Kate said stupidly.

Davis only continued to smile. "No, he is not, but if he's a friend of Richard Black's, then he's worth rescuing as well."

"Have you worked with Richard Black, the Duke of Lofton?" Jack asked her then .

Kate shook her head. "I've only worked with his son, the Earl of Stryden."

Jack shrugged. "You must have made an impression to warrant a rescue mission from the War Office in the midst of a war."

Kate looked at him. "This is unusual?" she asked.

Jack nodded. "Quite. We have intelligence that Murat's men are moving into position near Tolentino. To use a ship of the fleet in the region for purposes other than taking on Murat's men is highly unusual. So I wonder what it is that you did to warrant such rescue."

Kate frowned. "I suspect it's more to do with Thatcher. He is more well acquainted with the Blacks."

Jack nodded. "Now then , you had asked for a ship. I give you Captain Davis and his very capable vessel. What is it you have in mind?"

Kate looked to Captain Davis. "I plan to return to Naples

and rescue Matthew Thatcher by physical force from Scevola Amoretto."

Her statement was punctuated by the arrival of Mayhew with a tea cart. He steered in the direction of Jack, who pointed the man to the Salvatores, who still sat quietly on the sofa by the fireplace, Luigi having never removed his hands from their traveling cases.

Kate looked at Jack. "Do you know of any Salvatores in Palermo?" she asked him. "Rosa and Luigi have come to find their family who arrived in Sicily about three months ago."

Jack shook his head. "I do not, but I will be happy to ask around. The Salvatores are welcome to stay in residence until their family can be located."

For the first time since arriving at the commodore's residence, Luigi smiled. "Grazie," he said, nodding in Jack's direction.

Jack nodded curtly once in response as Mayhew left the room.

"Tell me about this Scevola man," Davis asked her.

Kate relayed the story of their failed mission involving Scevola's masked gala and her assumption that Thatcher must have made a deal with the man, Thatcher in exchange for safe passage for Kate and the Salvatores on one of Scevola's merchant ships. Davis nodded throughout her story and asked questions to clarify, but otherwise, he did not try to steer her.

When she had finished, Davis asked, "And how do we go about rescuing Mr. Thatcher?"

Kate looked at her feet. "I was hoping to storm Scevola's house with a contingent of the British fleet."

This brought a bark of laughter from Jack.

"Interesting plan, my lady," he said more calmly.

"I understand now that my plan may not warrant a

contingent of the British fleet, so I am open to suggestions," she said.

"I think what we need is a distraction," Davis said.

"How do you mean?" Jack asked, Kate's attention bouncing between the two of them.

"You said Scevola is quite wealthy," Davis said, looking to her. She nodded. "And with wealth comes concern for that wealth. Does Scevola have guards?"

Kate thought for a moment, remembering all of the costumed men that seemed to surround Scevola at the ball. She nodded. "I think he does."

Davis paced in front of the windows, his hands at his back as his peg leg clicked on the wooden floor.

"If you are to go in and take Thatcher by physical force, you will need a distraction to lure Scevola's men away from the house. Unless you think you're capable of taking on an entire league of trained guards?"

Kate shook her head once. "But what kind of distraction?"

Davis turned, his face screwing up into what could only be termed a smug sneer.

"What tis it that merchants fear most, me lady?" Davis said, and Kate did not recognize his voice, so completely and suddenly masked it was in some sort of brogue it had moments before not even exhibited. She shook her head again, her eyes growing wider as Captain Davis approached her, his hands behind his back, swinging his peg leg.

When he stood only feet in front of her, his smug sneer turned into a smile, and she thought he looked exactly like the next word he spoke.

"Pirates, me lady," he said, and Kate returned his smile.

CHAPTER 14

*T*he city of Naples lay in slumber, the moon but a whisper against the stucco facades of the houses and buildings, the red tile roofs sturdy nightcaps protecting those asleep inside. The air was still as the night and had not yet cooled enough for the wind to rush from the sea to the warmer hills above. All was quiet.

Too quiet.

Kate stood on the deck of Captain Reginald Davis' ship, her eyes scanning the hillside around Scevola's mansion. The hillside was dark except for the beacon that was the trader's ostentatiously lit residence. Torches bordered the promenade as well as the balcony above, and into the scrub of the hillside, she saw the winding path of lamps lighting the long road from town into the courtyard. The windows on the main floor of the house were dark, and the moon reflected off the panes in a blinding beam. But on the second story of the house, only two windows were warmed by a soft, yellow glow. It would be there that Kate would strike.

It was likely the windows on the balcony were actually

French doors that opened out, and Kate would be able to enter the house through one of those. She patted the pockets of her borrowed breeches for her lock-picking tools. It was a skill that came in handy only twice in her career, but she was thankful for the day Sarah Black, the Earl of Stryden's wife, had taught her the tricks necessary to unlatch locks. Ensuring that her tools were in place, she pulled on the brim of her dark hat, adjusting it so it covered her face with greater shadow. Her hair was tucked up underneath the garment, and with her breasts bound in linen and her shirt billowing to disguise the width of her hips, she looked rather like a man, which was the point. It wouldn't do if she were seen and discovered to be a woman on sight. Women had terrible reputations for being weaklings, and the guards were likely to give chase thinking her fun sport. The pistol tucked into the back of her pants precluded any concerns on this point. If anyone gave chase, she would just shoot him.

"The wind tis coming from the east tonight, me lady" Davis said as he stepped up beside her.

He had adopted his unusual brogue since they'd boarded the ship in Palermo, and Kate thought it suited him better than his defined tones of noted aristocracy. She wrinkled her brow at his words, not feeling any wind in the least, but as she was no sailor, she took his word for it.

"You'll be heading into it then as you take the hillside. A good omen," Davis said.

Kate nodded.

"The wind will carry any sound I make away from the house," she said, and Davis nodded.

"Are you prepared then ?"

Kate nodded, moving her toes about in her dark, sturdy boots, feeling the solid wood beneath her feet. She would need to be sure-footed tonight. Of that, she had no doubt.

"Let's be about it then ."

Davis gave out a call, and a dinghy dropped to the railing in front of her, held up by lines running into the rigging of the ship.

"I will wait for your signal," Davis said to Kate. "Before I send the first volley into the port. Are you sure about it then ?"

Kate took the lantern and flint a sailor standing by the dinghy offered to her. She nodded as she accepted them. "I'll give the signal when I reach shore."

"You then have exactly three quarters of an hour to complete your mission. I will intercept you at the rendezvous location. Is that clear, Agent Cavanaugh?"

She smiled at Davis. "Perfectly clear, Captain."

With one final nod, he helped Kate to board the dinghy. She adjusted herself on the seat and waited as the ropes lowered her into the water. As soon as she heard the splash down more than felt it, her hands gripped the oars in front of her, and she dropped the wooden paddles into the water. The sea was calm, a boon in her favor once more. It was a hundred yards to shore, and then an estimated fifty yards up scrabbly outcroppings to Scevola's hillside home. She gave the first shove against the oars, and the dinghy lurched forward.

She had three quarters of an hour.

The oars bit into the sea with vigor as each stroke moved her closer and closer to the shore. She had thought it too easy until she reached the push back at the shore's edge as the waves met the resistance of the land and flung themselves away, pushing back on her progress. But she leaned into it, throwing all of her nearly six foot frame against the oars. The small boat surged forward, and soon she felt the strike of dry land against the bottom of the vessel.

She scrambled out of the boat and with a single heave, brought it up on shore. For careful measure, she tied a rope from the boat to a scrubby tree along the shore. Pulling the lantern and flint from the boat, she knelt on the beach and quickly lit the lantern. It was a signaling lantern, surrounded on all sides by a moving metal shield. She carefully turned the opening toward the silent, dark mass sitting in the waters one hundred yards from shore. She carefully separated the metal shield, and a beam of light shot across the water, signaling the silent ship. Within moments, there came a resounding boom that ripped across the space as if nothing stood between her and the cannon the noise had erupted from. Quickly extinguishing the lantern, she pulled Commodore Lynwood's pocket watch from her breeches just as a tremendous splash rang through the port.

The apparent pirate attack on the city of Naples had begun, and she now had thirty-four minutes.

Tucking the watch carefully away, she adjusted the pistol in the back of her breeches and began the climb up the hillside. The outcroppings were coarse and sporadic. Her fingers scrambled to find purchase amongst rocks and boulders, her feet slipping in the gravel beneath them. Giving one last heave, she tumbled into the thicker growth surrounding Scevola's residence. She ducked, flattening herself against the ground, and listened as her racing heartbeat slowed after the exertion of the climb. When it was once more steady and solid, she began to crawl through the bushes.

She approached from the northwest, coming directly into the front of the house where the two windows beckoned with their warm glowing lights. She paused in the undergrowth, listening to the sounds of the house. It appeared silent, its occupants asleep, but Kate knew that could not be for long. A merchant like Scevola would recognize the sound of cannon fire, and he would send someone to investigate.

She was betting on the fact that Scevola himself was too much of a gentleman to go himself. But he would send men. And the more that left the house meant the fewer that remained to impede her way.

And just as she suspected, the main doors along the promenade burst open, and a dozen men ran out into the darkness. Her head swung around as the sounds of horses emerged from the other side of the house. The guards took up their reins, catapulting themselves into the saddles. They were gone as soon as she drew another breath, and the house fell silent once more, the two lit windows on the second floor calling to her.

Kate crouched and sidled more to the south, looking for a way to gain the second floor balcony. She rounded the corner of the house and stopped. There was a staircase leading from the second floor balcony to the ground, spilling into what looked to be a garden of sorts. She looked about her and began to move, only to freeze seconds later. Her eyes locked on the unmistakable glow of a lit cigar, the orange of its flame burning clearly through the darkness. There was someone at the base of the stairs in the courtyard, and he was enjoying a bit of tobacco. She paused, her breath slow and deep to avoid making undue noise. She waited, and as the wind shifted across her face, she caught the tang of its smoke. She waited again, and whoever it was that was smoking shuffled a few steps forward, coming away from the structure of the house into the moonlight.

He looked to be a young man of considerable build, and for a moment, her heart raced as she thought it was Thatcher. But it wasn't. It was one of Scevola's male guards. Waiting until the man turned away as if heading back towards the stairs, Kate moved. Her steps were light, delicate, and fast. She had struck the guard over the head with the butt of her pistol even before he drew the next puff of his cigar. He dropped to the ground in a pitiful slump. Kate stomped on the cigar.

"Disgusting habit," she murmured, wrinkling her nose.

Pressing her back to the stucco of the house, she made her way up the staircase, crisscrossing her legs one in front of the other to keep as flat against the wall as possible. When she neared the top, she slowed, listening. The murmur of voices reached her ears, and she stopped entirely, dropping slowly to the risers of the stairs. She pressed herself against them, keeping the exposed white skin of her face down and away to avoid detection. She listened.

Voices, or rather a single voice, traveled the length of the balcony, but the voice did not alter as if its owner were approaching. Whoever it was that spoke was stationary somewhere along the length of the balcony. Kate raised her head and crawled the remainder of the stairs, her head poking above the landing just enough to see the empty balcony stretch before her. The voice was clearer now, and she could tell it came from a room off of the balcony. She strained forward, her head tilting enough to see in the direction of the lit windows. She saw it then , the small crack between panes indicating the presence of a door.

A door left ajar.

Rising into a crouch, Kate silently crossed the length of the balcony until she stood outside of the open doors. And she waited, listening to the beat of her heart slow as she took in the words being said beyond the open doors.

It was Scevola.

And he was speaking English.

* * *

CANNON FIRE.

As any good merchant, Scevola knew the sound and

could recall the instant sensation of dread that passed through him at its call. He did not show his reaction in any way, however, especially as he had company in his bedchamber that evening. Instead of rushing to the doors of the balcony, he had simply walked to the bell pull in the corner of the room, summoned his butler, and when the man arrived, gave him instructions to send several men down to the port to see what was happening.

There had only been a single shot as of then , and he would not allow such an event to prevent him from enjoying the night's planned festivities. He drank the last of his brandy as he heard the sounds of horses retreating in the direction of the port. No more cannon fire had sounded, and he allowed himself to focus on more important factors. He turned away from the drink cart after refilling his glass, holding the drink high and shaking it slightly in the direction of his companion.

"Are you sure you do not wish to enjoy a fine brandy, Mr. Thatcher?" he asked.

The American did not move or indicate in any way that he had heard Scevola.

He only said, "I would not care for a drink."

His words were clipped, his tone flat, but Scevola knew that he could change that soon. It would only take time for the man to relax. It was always like this with the new ones, and they always relaxed. Always.

Swirling the liquor about in his glass, he strolled over to Thatcher, his bare toes sinking into the plush carpet that covered most of the floor in his bedchamber. Despite the warmth of the night, he had had a fire built, and it crackled and popped just as he liked it when he wanted an air of romance in the room. His chosen conquest did not suggest that he was affected by such measures, but Scevola enjoyed it nonetheless.

He stopped in front of Thatcher, and the folds of his silk dressing gown swished between his bare legs. Taking a single finger, he lifted it to the American's bare chest, running it through the thick springs of hair there and down to the chiseled muscles of his abdomen. The American did not flinch at his touch, and Scevola took this as a good sign. Smiling, he turned about again, making his way over to the chair in front of the open doors. He would have preferred to sit in front of the fire, but it was over warm in the room already, and what breeze came through the doors would help to cool him. He sat, splaying his legs wide, regardless of how the folds of his dressing gown may fall or what may be exposed to his companion. He intended everything to be exposed to his companion by night's end.

"And how is it that you find yourself in Naples, young friend?" he asked, sipping from his glass.

Thatcher did not respond right away, so Scevola raised an eyebrow, the only impetus needed to remind the man that they had made a deal, and an arrangement was struck.

"State business," Thatcher said.

Scevola smiled. "So many sins can fall under such a word. What sort of state business?"

For the first time, the American made an involuntary move, belying his true feelings. It was a twitch of muscle along his jaw, and Scevola scanned the rest of the man, hoping to see more as he ran his gaze from his bared chest to the snug fitting breeches and bared feet. But nothing else about his person gave any hint as to what he was feeling.

But Scevola had his suspicions. When he had first encountered the man, there had been no hope of luring him into his employ, so he was more than a bit startled when the man showed up on his doorstep within days, asking to speak with him about his offer. He hadn't recalled until that moment that he had made any such offer, but when he had seen who it was, his features recognizable even without his golden mask, Scevola could recall only too well what offer he had made the gentleman. And to see him here now, standing half undressed in his bedchamber, Scevola was very pleased that he had thought to make such an offer.

However, Thatcher had struck the deal with a willingness Scevola did not often see in men, and as he had already determined it was not a natural inclination for the male sex that had brought him back, he knew it must have been something far greater. He had seen the woman standing on the deck of his ship when it had pulled away from the pier. He had heard her declaration of love, and for but a moment, Scevola wondered what that must be like. For someone to love another so deeply that he would sacrifice himself and in exchange, listen to the heartbreaking cry of the one he loved.

Most interesting, indeed.

But business was business, and a deal had been made. He had provided passage to the three refugees without question, concealing them on his merchant vessel bound for Sicily. It was Thatcher's turn to hold up his end of the bargain. He listened again for a moment, but no more cannon fire had sounded. He drew a deep breath and let his mind focus on the delectable situation at hand.

"I think it's time that you got more comfortable, Mr. Thatcher," Scevola said, setting his glass down on a table as he sat up in his chair, adjusting his shoulders against the back so he had a better view of his companion. "Perhaps removing your pants would help."

He waited for Thatcher to comply, but instead he heard the unmistakable sound of a pistol being cocked directly beside his right ear.

He did not move. He did not speak. He listened to the sound of his heart pick up its pace and waited.

"I believe Mr. Thatcher will be keeping his pants on, Scevola," came a voice to his immediate right.

A very feminine voice.

Keeping his eyes on Thatcher, Scevola let a smile come to his lips.

"The scorned woman returns. What a nice twist."

Now he did move, but only his head as he turned to get a better look as his presumed assassin. He would have been astounded at the woman's attire if he had not seen far worse in his life. She was dressed from hat to boots in black, men's breeches and lawn shirt, her figure disguised so only her height gave clue to her person, a false clue suggesting she were a man.

"And she's come in costume. How lovely," he said.

He looked back at Thatcher.

"I suppose our deal is off then. Your lady love is once more in Naples, and I clearly failed to do my part."

Thatcher did not move, his face blank of expression. The poor man was likely stupefied at the sudden appearance of the golden woman from the San Gennaro ball. Scevola had to admit she looked far better dressed as a man than in that awful golden contraption she had been in that night. With Thatcher unmoving and his only other opponent a woman, Scevola thought a moment about his options. Thatcher was a fine acquisition, but he had had better and would likely have better still. It would do him no good to expend any resources on keeping him. Especially if the woman did something stupid like shoot him.

The boom of cannon fire sounded through the balcony doors once more, and he smiled even harder.

"I assume that is your conveyance which is plaguing my port of call?" he asked, moving only his eyes to the woman beside him.

She nodded. "Quite."

He thought of the cargo he had held in port waiting for departure the next morning. The cost was high, and even the satisfaction of his carnal pleasure could not make up for it.

"I see then. Mr. Thatcher, I must insist that you leave at once. You are not worth the destruction of the cargo on my ships in port. It was terribly distracting for a time, but now I must say good bye to you."

Thatcher seemed to hesitate, but then he moved in the direction of the balcony doors, making no contact with the woman holding the pistol at Scevola's head. As Thatcher slipped between the open doors, disappearing from view, Scevola slowly rose, keeping his actions checked so as not to startle the woman into shooting him.

"Well played, madam," he said, turning fully to face her.

"Thank you," she said and had the gall to smirk at him.

He felt the sting of his pride, but at the same moment, he also felt a sense of fair defeat. "And what it is that I say when asked how I was unmanned?"

Leveling the pistol at his chest, she said, "You tell them Katharine Cavanaugh came calling."

And with that, she disappeared into the night.

* * *

KATE RAN to the stairs at the end of the balcony. Thatcher stood at the top of them, a hand outstretched, waiting for her to take it. She tucked her pistol into the back of her breeches as she took Thatcher's hand. They descended the stairs quickly, the footfalls silent as they hit the paving stones that led into the gardens beyond. Thatcher halted suddenly, and she looked up.

Three guards stood in front of them, and each of them had his gaze locked on them. It appeared the one she had incapacitated on her way up the stairs had been found by two comrades. The one still held a hand pressed to the back of his head, but he dropped it when he spotted her. He shouted something at her in a language she didn't understand, but she didn't retreat. She threw a sidelong glance at Thatcher, who very carefully cast a glance behind them.

Kate, with equal stealth, also looked behind them before she snapped her gaze forward at the three guards approaching them.

"Mr. Thatcher, would you care to dance?" she said.

"I reckon I would," Thatcher said.

Together, they stepped back in one fluid motion, grasping the arms of a wooden bench that sat behind them. Together, they heaved it into the air, running forward as they did so. The bench connected with the three guards in a sickening blow, knocking them to the ground. Kate felt the blow ricochet up her arms, but she didn't lose her grip on the piece of furniture until she and Thatcher had cleared the men.

Dropping the bench, they took off at a run in the direction of the hillside only to find a guard returning on horseback, galloping along the drive. Kate thought they could make it to the scrub in time, but suddenly, horse and rider were upon them, shouting again in a language she didn't understand. She turned reflexively, raising her arms in the universal symbol of surrender.

The guard trained a pistol at her, and she lost track of where Thatcher was. When the gunshot split the night air, her eyes shuttered, not wanting to see the blood blooming along her chest, or worse, see Thatcher fall to the ground beside her. When she opened her eyes, she saw Thatcher standing beside her, the pistol that had been tucked into the back of her breeches hanging at his side, smoking from recently being shot. She swung her gaze to find the horse before her empty of its rider.

"Well done, Mr. Thatcher," she said.

He tipped an invisible hat in her direction. "Thank you, ma'am," he said.

"We need to hurry."

She grabbed his arm, pulling him in the direction of the scrub along the hillside. Soon they burst onto the beach below, Kate's feet digging into the sand and pushing off. She threw herself into the dingy waiting on the shore, pulling the rope free from the tree she had tied it to earlier. The boat beneath her began to move as Thatcher shoved off, launching himself into the boat and picking up the oars in a single motion.

Kate dug at the pocket of her breeches, pulling Commodore Lynwood's pocket watch free.

Twelve minutes.

* * *

THE OARS of the dinghy splashed into the sea as Thatcher's muscles coiled with the tension to pull the paddles through the water. Kate sat in the bow in front of him, her face turned in the direction of port. He saw a ship as it trailed away from the wharf, its bulk blocking most of the town beyond it. But he clearly saw the bodies, small from this distance, scurrying about the web of docks at the wharf, trying to gain purchase on ships, readying sails to get the ships out of port. Thatcher suddenly realized the reason for the sounds of cannon fire earlier.

"You brought pirates to rescue me?"

Kate shook her head but didn't look at him. She appeared to be looking at a watch in her hand. "Not exactly," she said.

When she finally turned to look at Thatcher, the moon-light illuminated her like a Greek goddess as her hair had come free of its cap and flowed behind her in a wave. His heart thudded against his ribcage at the sight of her. He had thought he would never see her again.

"I asked Katharine Cavanaugh what she wanted," she said then , her voice serious, her face stern.

Thatcher smiled slowly, feeling every fold of each muscle on his face.

"You did?" he asked.

"It turns out she wants you. If you'll have her," she said.

Her words struck him as if they carried physical weight, and he felt his heart pick up speed. But where before he would have dreaded, feared even, such a connection with another human being, he could not imagine living without Kate now. He knew the reality of what a life without her would be like. He had lived it for twenty-four hours. And twenty-four hours was longer than he had needed to realize nothing would be worse than living without Katharine Cavanaugh.

"Is that so?" he said, "I reckon I'll have her then ."

She smiled, but soon her face changed into a look so dark he had not seen the like on her face before then .

"And the next time you get a brilliant idea like this during one of our missions, I'll ask you to share it with me before executing it. Am I clear, Mr. Thatcher?" she said.

Now Thatcher raised an eyebrow at her. "Our missions?" he asked.

Kate raised an eyebrow in return, which earned a laugh from Thatcher. "Do you not wish to be partners with Captain Hadley's daughter? I hear she's quite the agent."

"I'd rather be partners with Katharine Cavanaugh," he said.

She smiled and looked back in the direction of the oncoming ship before looking back down at the watch in her hand. "Kate?" he asked, wondering what she was about.

"Keep rowing toward that ship," she said, not turning to look at him.

"Kate," he said again, but this time more sternly.

She turned to look at him.

"I love you, too," he said.

She smiled at him and said, "Keep rowing."

The dinghy all but ran into the oncoming ship as lines came down around them, and sailors seemed to drop from the air, rigging the dinghy for lift. Without stepping from the small vessel, the entire thing rose into the air. Kate held onto the side as they swung through the night until the railing appeared once more in view. Thatcher reached out a hand to her, helping her to board the ship. When his bare feet touched the solid wood of the ship's deck, he felt a tension seep from his shoulders he had not known he had been holding in. A man approached them then , who by all appearances, was indeed a pirate.

"So this is the Mr. Thatcher I've been sent all this way to rescue."

Thatcher looked about him at the men manning the lines and deck, garbed in cut off breeches and ragged shirts, sporting bandanas tied about their heads. He leaned into Kate. "I thought you were bringing the British navy," he whispered.

"This is the British navy," she whispered back.

Thatcher raised an eyebrow. "Then the crown may wish to rethink expenditures on uniforms," he murmured.

"I would say the same about you, laddie," the man said, gesturing towards Thatcher's lack of clothing.

Kate gestured between the two men. "Captain Davis," she said, "Mr. Thatcher."

Thatcher nodded in introduction at the captain.

"Very pleased to make your acquaintance," Thatcher said,

once more reaching for his hat that was once again lost to him.

Kate interrupted the introductions, saying to the captain, "I have further need of your services."

The captain tilted his head in question. "We've rescued the bloke. What more do ye need, lassie?"

Kate reached out and grabbed Thatcher's bare arm, pulling him against her. "Marry us," she said.

"What?" Thatcher said at the same time Davis said, "Marry you?"

Looking between Thatcher and Davis, Kate answered Davis first.

"Yes, marry us. You're a captain of the British navy, and as a captain of this vessel, maritime law states that you can marry us. So I ask that you marry us. Right now," she added, being as precise as he would expect of Kate Cavanaugh.

Thatcher pulled at the arm she held. "Kate, what are you doing?" he asked.

She latched onto his arm harder than he thought possible, but he resisted. He did not want her making some rash decision because once he made a choice to negotiate a bargain that included them being separated forever. And worse, he didn't want her to make such a life altering decision in a moment of heightened tension. But as Kate always was, she was persistent.

"I told you. I know what Katharine Cavanaugh wants," she said, turning her sudden fury on him, "I want you, Matthew Thatcher, and if you ever do something so stupid again, so help me God!"

He waited, expecting more of her rant, but perhaps the anticipation of the rescue or the pent up anxiety at their separation or everything she had likely felt for the past twenty years of her life suddenly overwhelmed her, and Thatcher stood there watching the great Captain Hadley's daughter splutter at him. Thatcher carefully freed his arm to take her shoulders in his hands.

"This is what Katharine Cavanaugh wants?" he asked, his casual grin coming to his face, hoping it would ease her clearly rattled nerves.

"Yes," she said, her voice steady now.

Thatcher looked at the captain.

"You heard the woman. I reckon I'm getting married."

CHAPTER 15

ondon, England
August 1815

KATE WALKED through the front door of her London townhouse, letting the scents of freshly polished wood and scrubbed floors assail her at the entrance. Thatcher came in behind her, removing his hat, and letting out a low whistle as he entered the room.

"I reckon I married well," he said, his gaze scanning the marble floors of the front hall and the mahogany staircase that rose up to the floors above.

She smiled at him, removing her hat and gloves to set them on the front hall table.

"I reckon you did," she said.

He bent and quickly kissed her, the touch of his lips still new and exhilarating even after more than three months of marriage. At the sound of an inordinately feminine screech behind them, Kate stepped back to find her butler staring at her, eyes wide and jaw hung low.

"My lady!" he exclaimed. "What has happened to your face?"

He pointed at said body part, and Kate merely smiled.

"It's called a tan, Banks, and it is no longer my lady. It is Mrs. Thatcher. And may I introduce Mr. Thatcher," she said, casting a hand in the direction of her husband.

She was sure her butler was about to expire at her feet, but she ignored it.

After they had learned the location of the Salvatores upon their return to Palermo, she and Thatcher had decided they had earned a bit of a wedding trip. They rented a house near the Salvatores, intending to stay only a few weeks, but a few weeks had turned into a few months. With Napoleon on his way out, thanks to Wellington's brilliant handling at Waterloo, the War Office had not deemed it necessary for Kate to make a hasty retreat to London. So she and Thatcher enjoyed Palermo and the Salvatores, none of which were babies, although Rosa insisted that they were, and especially the private rooftop portico of their rented home outside of Palermo. If Banks knew how much of her was tanned, the man would die of an apoplectic fit.

"What strange ways you must have endured in Palermo," Banks said then , stepping aside to allow them to enter. "Mr. Thatcher, welcome," he finished.

"Thank you," Thatcher drawled, stepping around Kate to shake Banks' hand. "It's a real pleasure."

And then Banks did expire, Kate was sure of it. She couldn't help the snort of laughter that burbled its way up, and she attempted to cover it with a clearing of her throat.

Kate said, "Banks, will you send for Cook to meet me in my study?"

Banks nodded, his wide eyes never straying from Thatcher, and said, "Cook has taken care of the menu for the week, my- Mrs. Thatcher. You needn't worry--"

"It's not the menu," Kate cut him off. "I wish to speak with Cook about acquiring the necessary tools for me to make pasta in the kitchen."

And if Banks had died when Thatcher had shaken his hand, Kate was certain then that Banks believed he had entered Bedlam itself.

"The kitchens, ma'am? You want to...cook?"

Kate nodded, moving in the direction of her study.

"Yes, Banks, I wish to cook. So please send her along immediately."

She waved the servant off with a casual flick of her hand and noticed Thatcher smiling at her as she entered her study. The room was just as she had left it with its rose draperies, cream upholstery, and shelves of books. The post was laid out on her rosewood desk on the far side of the room, and she made her way to it.

"Charming," Thatcher said, looking about the room as she picked up the first pile of outdated invitations.

As she sifted through the post, it became apparent that she had missed quite an exciting season if the volume and quality of the invitations on her desk were anything to judge it by. She looked up briefly to find Thatcher studying the shelves and the contents of her library. She smiled at how at ease he looked in her home. She had never thought to be nervous or to wonder what he would think upon their return to London. She had no attachments to her townhouse, or London for that matter, and would be happy to follow him anywhere as long as she had access to a kitchen well stocked with pots and pans and proper cutlery.

"I must alert the Office as to our return," she said.

Thatcher made a noise that he had heard her, his finger scanning the spines of books.

"Will they assign us a mission so quickly upon our return?"

Kate shrugged, even though he wasn't looking at her.

"I'm not sure. With Napoleon out of the way, I'm not sure who it is that the Office would have us spy on."

Thatcher turned toward her, his wicked grin wide on his face. "Maybe we'll get to spy on the Americans," he said, and she snorted a laugh.

"Hardly," she said and returned to the post in her hands.

She paused in her sorting when she noticed a pristine envelope on the edge of her desk. It was blank except for her name printed carefully across the face. It had all the markings of a War Office missive. Kate picked it up carefully, running it between her fingers, a frown wrinkling her forehead. She had spoken the truth when she had told Thatcher she would need to alert the War Office as to their return as no one in the Office knew when she was expected to arrive in London. She slid her finger under the flap to open it. The post inside indicated today's date. She frowned harder. The note must have been delivered that morning. She quickly scanned the letter and felt her very life drain away.

She must have sat down or likely fallen down because Thatcher was suddenly in front of her, his big hands on her shoulders, shaking her slightly as she heard him ask if she were all right, but his words were muffled and didn't make sense. She stared at him, the letter forgotten in her lap.

"It's not the Americans we'll need to worry about. There's a mole in the spy network," she said, her voice barely above a whisper, her gaze focused on the bright blue eyes of her husband.

"How do you know?" Thatcher asked.

She held up the letter.

"The Duke of Lofton has been killed."

ABOUT THE AUTHOR

Jessie decided to be a writer because the job of Indiana Jones was already filled.

Taking her history degree dangerously, Jessie tells the stories of courageous heroines, the men who dared to love them, and the world that tried to defeat them.

Jessie makes her home in the great state of New Hampshire where she lives with her husband and two very opinionated Basset hounds. For more, visit her website at jessieclever.com.